FINDING

Yvonne

Also by Brandy Colbert

Pointe

Little & Lion

FINDING

Yvonne

BRANDY COLBERT

LITTLE, BROWN AND COMPANY
New York   Boston

Little, Brown and Company
Hachette Book Group
1290 Avenue of the Americas, New York, NY 10104
Visit us at LBYR.com

First Edition: August 2018

Little, Brown and Company is a division of Hachette Book Group, Inc. The Little, Brown name and logo are trademarks of Hachette Book Group, Inc.

The publisher is not responsible for websites (or their content) that are not owned by the publisher.

Library of Congress Cataloging-in-Publication Data
Names: Colbert, Brandy, author.
Title: Finding Yvonne / by Brandy Colbert.
Description: First edition. | New York : Little, Brown and Company, 2018. |
Summary: Raised by a workaholic father who is a restauranteur, Yvonne, eighteen, faces difficult choices about love, her training as a violinist, college, and career as high school graduation draws near.
Identifiers: LCCN 2017020284 | ISBN 9780316349055 (hardcover) |
ISBN 9780316349062 (ebook)
Subjects: | CYAC: Fathers and daughters—Fiction. | Single-parent families—Fiction. | Dating (Social customs)—Fiction. | Restaurants—Fiction. | Violinists—Fiction. | African Americans—Fiction.
Classification: LCC PZ7.C66998 Fin 2018 | DDC [Fic]—dc23
LC record available at https://lccn.loc.gov/2017020284

ISBNs: 978-0-316-34905-5 (hardcover), 978-0-316-34906-2 (ebook)

Printed in the United States of America

LSC-C

10 9 8 7 6 5 4 3 2 1

For the girls who are still searching

PART 1.

1.

There are three things I know about my father:
He smokes pot daily, he doesn't like to speak unless
he really has something to say, and he is one of the most
respected chefs in Los Angeles.

I also know that the best time to see him is at Sunday
breakfast. We aren't around each other much; Dad gets home
from work so late during the week that he's rarely up in time
to make a proper breakfast. He usually grabs something
light when he gets up, around noon, and then eats family
meal with the staff before the restaurant opens for dinner.
But Sundays are special. He reserves Sunday mornings for
an actual meal that he plans in advance, and there's always
plenty to eat.

Sometimes I want to skip it on principle alone. I shouldn't have to set aside one day a week to see my own dad for more than a few minutes. But I love Sunday breakfast, and he's usually in a good mood because he gets the day to himself, so I find myself at the table every week.

He's standing at the counter when I stumble into the kitchen this morning, coating pieces of chicken in a mixture of flour and seasonings.

"Morning," he says over his shoulder. "Coffee's on."

"Thanks." I pour a mug and stand next to the fridge, watching him. "Is Warren coming over?"

"Should be here any minute."

Which means I'll need to down this cup of coffee if I want to brush my teeth again before he gets here. I slurp steadily at the mug, but the doorbell rings before I can finish. Well, it's not like anything is going to happen with my father here.

Warren Engel is standing on the porch in jeans and a plaid button-down with the sleeves rolled up. He smiles and wordlessly reaches for my hands. I pull him inside and we stand looking at each other for a moment, his big tea-colored eyes roaming softly over me before we hug.

"Missed you last night," he says in a low voice, though Dad couldn't hear us over all the banging around he's doing in the kitchen anyway.

"Sorry I didn't make it over. The party went late, and then I just wanted to sleep in my own bed."

"It's cool. I was at the restaurant until late." Warren was promoted to sous chef at my father's restaurant a couple of months ago, a big honor in itself but especially since he's just barely twenty-one. "What's Sinclair making today?"

"Come see for yourself," I say, leading him back through the hallway. His hands trail lightly over my hips as we walk, sending warm shivers up the small of my back, but it ends as quickly as it started. We break apart when we're standing in the same room as my father.

We're not official, Warren and I. We probably would be if he weren't so paranoid about our age difference. We're only three years apart, and I don't think my father would care. He basically thinks Warren can do no wrong.

Dad is carefully placing chicken legs and thighs into a skillet of hot oil as we walk in.

"Chicken and waffles?" Warren says, grinning like the day just turned into Christmas. My father has a lot of fans, known and unknown, but I think Warren might still be his biggest.

"You know it." My father moves the skillet to a cool burner. "Want to get the waffles going? Iron's already hot, and the batter's in the fridge."

I reach into the refrigerator to hand Warren the pitcher of

batter, then grab the jug of orange juice, too. "Isn't he off the clock?"

"Happy to let you take over if you're so concerned about Warren," Dad says, smirking as he heads over to the sunroom.

Not two minutes later, the skunky scent of marijuana wafts through the air above us. Neither Warren nor I bat an eye. My father's frequent pot-smoking isn't exactly public knowledge, but it's certainly no secret around here. He says it's mostly to combat the stress that comes with owning a successful restaurant, but he also swears that he's created some of his most iconic dishes while stoned. He probably knows that I've smoked, but we don't talk about it and we've certainly never done so together.

Dad is what I call a professional stoner. He's been smoking for so long that it's hard to tell when he's high. The whites of his eyes turn just slightly pink, and sometimes he takes a little longer between thoughts, but other than that he's completely functional. Almost disturbingly so. I've seen him carry on extremely involved conversations when I know he's blazed up pretty recently.

I down a glass of orange juice while Warren tends to the waffles, creating a generous stack on a plate next to the chicken. Dad comes back in just as they're ready, and we all help transport everything to the table. I carry plates and silverware and quickly set the table as they place the food.

Eating with my father and Warren isn't like sharing a meal with anyone else I've ever known. Usually people taste a few bites of their food, declare how good it is or what it's lacking, then move on to more stimulating conversation. Warren and my dad analyze each bite, discussing which spices were or were not used and what they've changed since the last time they made the meal. Sometimes Dad gives him tips on his method, but I realized how much he respects Warren when he started asking for his opinion.

I grew up in the restaurant industry, but I don't understand food the way they do. Except for sweets. Baking makes sense to me, maybe because there's science behind it. There's so much trial and error with cooking. I get frustrated when a recipe doesn't turn out right the first time, even when I follow it to the letter.

"I was thinking about going to check out that new spot in Venice," Dad says to Warren. "The one Courtney Winters just opened up."

"Oh, that place is supposed to be the real deal." Warren wipes his mouth and takes a long drink of water. "You're going today?"

"She has a Sunday supper. What do you think?"

"Yeah, sure." Warren pauses and looks at my dad first, then me. "You want to come?"

I pour more syrup over my waffle and take a bite. Even I

can't help but stop and think how perfectly light and fluffy it is as I chew. "I don't know," I say, looking at my father. "Am I invited?"

"Of course you are, Yvonne. I thought you'd be practicing," Dad says with a shrug.

I do usually practice my violin on Sunday. It feels like a good end to the weekend. A structured start to the week. But I need a break from the routine sometimes. And now that I'm no longer taking private lessons, I can make my own practice schedule.

"Can we stop at the boardwalk?"

"Yeah, sure." Dad waves one hand in the air as he drags a forkful of chicken and waffles through a pool of syrup with the other. He's already done with this conversation, ready to get back to food talk.

The meal with them tonight will be almost exactly like the scene at this kitchen table, only they'll sample an unreasonable amount of food, and my father will go back to the kitchen to talk to the chef, and I'll have to hear everything from why he thinks the dining-room sconces are incompatible with the space to him breaking down the components of a sauce.

It's exhausting, but I know the meal will be good. My father won't try just anyone's food. And I'll get to spend time with Warren, which always makes me happy. He works such long hours that we don't get to see each other as often as I'd like.

Besides, I don't have anything else to do today. My Sundays used to be filled with violin practice, but with Denis no longer around to crack the whip, I don't see much of a point.

It's hard not to give up on yourself when the person who's supposed to believe in you the most already has.

2.

My geology teacher, Mr. Gamble, used to live in Venice Beach before we were born, and he says none of us would have survived it back then. He says the streets were full of gangs and crumbling bungalows and people addicted to crack.

Gentrification has changed a lot of that, but luckily the boardwalk has remained as weird as ever. One area is devoted to shirtless meatheads who like to lift weights in front of tourists, the aptly named Muscle Beach. Then there's the section where the skaters take turns braving the terrifying maze of concrete ramps on their boards.

But my favorite part is walking down the pavement-lined path that stretches by booths of tie-dyed clothing, shops hawking cheap souvenirs, and doctors who will prescribe medical-marijuana cards in thirty minutes. There are places to grab a drink or a bite to eat, and on the other side is the ocean, separated only by the art vendors, the street performers, and the wide expanse of sand.

Salt water and incense and competing strains of weed fill the air as I stroll down the boardwalk between Warren and my dad. My father's phone rings and he looks down at the screen, says he has to take it and he'll catch up with us.

Warren and I walk so that our arms occasionally bump into each other, but no closer than that. I think he's afraid my dad will freak out if he ever sees us touching, but I keep telling him he's paranoid. My father knows there's something between Warren and me, even if there's no label. The fact that I spend the night at Warren's place so often and Dad never says anything about it should reassure him more than it does.

"Would you ever live over here?" Warren asks as we pass a table full of heavy silver jewelry displayed on black velvet.

"I don't know." I wrap my arms around myself. The beach is always noticeably cooler than the rest of the city. It feels like we're not even in Los Angeles, the temperature has changed so much from when we left Highland Park. "It's so different. And I'd pretty much need to be a billionaire to rent an apartment."

"You're so practical." He nudges me gently. "If money

were no object and you could live anywhere in the city in your dream house—could you live in Venice?"

"I guess the beach is nice, but I like where we live better," I say. "I couldn't handle so many tourists."

"It's probably easy to avoid them when you know your way around." He pauses. "I think I could hang at the beach."

"You're not allowed to move this far away from me," I say, shaking my head. "I'd never see you."

"You mean not until you leave next year?" Warren's voice is more matter-of-fact than accusatory.

Still, it makes me wince. I've been trying not to think about the fact that there will probably be a day when we don't live in the same city. Even if I don't go to an out-of-state school, there's a chance Warren could move on himself. He could get scooped up by another chef when my father isn't paying attention. Or he could just move somewhere else to start his own restaurant, which he'll inevitably do one day.

"That's a whole year away. And we don't even know what's going to happen."

He doesn't say anything else about it, and I'm trying to figure out what to say to bring the mood back up when I hear the strings.

If cooking is my father's and Warren's thing, music has always been mine. Dad got me my first violin about a year after my mother left, when I was seven. We tried a few different activities—I guess so I wouldn't spend all my free time wondering why I suddenly had no mother: dance lessons, Girl Scouts, classes at a local children's theater. None of it stuck, but as soon as we walked into the violin shop, which was also filled with beautiful violas and cellos that seemed absolutely monstrous at the time, I felt right at home. Even the shop owner, whose deep frown made it clear that he didn't like children getting too close to the merchandise, said nothing as I walked around slowly, staring in awe at the instruments.

My elementary-school orchestra teacher, Ms. Francine, told me I had a gift for music. She didn't say I was the best in the orchestra or even the best in the violin section, but I never forgot what she said. I never told anyone, though. I had been taking private lessons with Denis for a couple of years by the time I started playing in her orchestra. I only realized recently that maybe I wanted that praise all to myself because I didn't want anyone to taint it. People are always telling my father how great he is at what he does—one of the best—but that was the first time anyone had said that to me, and I didn't want the validation taken away. Even then, I knew I had to be protective of it; I've never stood out for anything besides violin.

Coaxing bittersweet melodies from the strings of my instrument has always been satisfying, but performing has never given me the same thrill as listening to other people play.

The music is coming from a guy and a girl at the edge of the boardwalk. A crowd stands in front of them, but it's a small group. No more than a dozen people tapping their feet on the pavement, leaning closer to better hear the notes. The makeshift audience is trying to place the song, but if anyone knows it, I can't tell. Most of them stand there with bemused but pleasant expressions on their faces, as if they were unaware that such music could come from string instruments.

I put my hand on Warren's arm so he'll stop. He looks confused at first, then nods as he sees them. We stand silently, and I let the notes of the old song soar through my ears and into me. Sometimes I hear songs that I like, that are interesting or catchy enough for me to take notice as I'm doing homework or getting ready for the day. Then there are melodies that seep into me, winding through every part of my body with such intensity that I can't do anything but sit still and listen. It's not always the song itself; sometimes it's a certain variation or the musician's individual stamp that resonates. I can't pinpoint what it is about the music I'm listening to now, but all I want to do is close my eyes and let it settle into me.

The girl's arms are long and graceful as she strikes the bow with confidence against the strings of her viola. The guy's sandaled foot keeps beat on the ground, barely visible beneath the tattered hem of his wrinkled pants. He's playing a battered violin as beautifully as if he were standing onstage at

Carnegie Hall with a shiny new instrument. He catches my eye through the space between people, and it makes my heart thrum its own distinct rhythm in my chest. I stare back at him for too long before I turn to Warren.

"So good, right?" I whisper, though it's not like we're at a concert. The boardwalk is very much still the boardwalk, with children darting back and forth and people shouting and the commotion around the other performers cutting through the music. But I know what it's like to perform, when you want to think people are really listening, taking in every single note that you've been practicing for months.

Warren pretends to consider this, tilting his head to the side and squinting at the musicians. "You're better," he finally whispers back.

I'm not, but I like hearing it, so I keep my mouth closed. Besides, I don't want to miss any more of them. I thought I would recognize the song by now, but it's a tune on the tip of my tongue, a melody I still can't place. I'm jealous that they get to play contemporary—it's classical or bust with Ms. Ortiz in the school orchestra. Denis felt the same way.

They finish to a smattering of applause. Some people drop money into a hat placed in front of them. Others sort of stare for a while before wandering off, on to the next person or thing that will hold their attention for a few moments. Soon it's just me standing a few feet in front of them, and I'm trying to get up the nerve to say something, but I don't know what.

"What's wrong?"

Warren. I'd forgotten he was still here, right next to me.

"Nothing," I say, though my heart still isn't beating normally.

"You look out of it."

I shake my head, then turn back to the musicians. The guy picks up the hat and hands it to the girl, who quickly counts the money and drops it into a small canvas bag at her feet. They exchange a few words, and whoever they are to each other, it looks easy between them. I can't tell if they're brother and sister or if they're together, but I keep staring, trying to figure it out. I don't realize how long I've been looking at them without the barrier of people between us until the guy turns back to replace the hat and stares right at me.

"Can I help you out with something?" His voice is softer than I imagined.

"Oh—I—just, um, you—you're very good." I reach for my purse until I remember I left it in the car. My pockets are empty. I nudge Warren.

He sighs, but digs into his jeans pocket and hands me a couple of bills. I walk forward and drop them into the hat. I'm embarrassed, acting like the type of tourist they must see every day, but I don't know what else to say. Do I admit that their playing enchanted me? That it's been a long time since music, especially strings, has made me feel this way?

The guy is cute, which doesn't help my inability to form another sentence. He has tawny skin and broad shoulders with a head of thick brown dreadlocks that fall past them. I like looking at him, but it's not just that. There's an electric feeling I can't ignore, a charge pulsing through the air as I stand close to him. As if a part of me I didn't know was sleeping has suddenly awakened.

"Thanks, sis," he says, then nods at Warren. He smiles at me before he turns around to talk to the girl, who has a mass of tightly curled hair pulled up into an Afro puff. She's busy wiping the chin rest of her viola with a rag.

"We should find Sinclair." Warren briefly puts his hand on my elbow, snapping me out of my daze. "Maybe head over to the restaurant?"

"Yeah, sure." I turn to go with him, but look back over my shoulder.

Warren tugs at my arm. "Yvonne, seriously, is everything okay?"

When I glance over, he's looking back and forth between them and me, trying to figure out what just happened. Warren and I don't spend a lot of time with other people when we're together, and it occurs to me that it's been a while since he's seen me with another guy. I don't know if he's ever seen me with one who intrigues me like this. There's a bit of jealousy mixed with the bewilderment in his eyes.

"I'm fine." My voice comes out thin and unsure. Not very convincing.

Warren is still watching me. I smile to ease his worry and let him pull me away, back into the pulsing throng of beachgoers.

We took two cars down to the beach, so after dinner Warren and I go off on our own. He drives us back to his neighborhood.

"There's a full moon tonight," he says, pointing out the window when we pull up to a stoplight. "Want to take a look?"

We wind along Silver Lake Boulevard, parking on a side street near the reservoir. The sky darkened on our way back from Venice, but people are still walking along the path. A few are running around in the dusty dog park, tossing balls to their pets.

"What was all that stuff earlier about living in Venice?" I ask as we begin our walk. There aren't many people on this section of the pathway.

"I don't know." Warren shrugs. "Sometimes I think about the future. Don't you?"

"Of course." Except it scares me to think about it too much because I'm not sure I know what I want. "But I don't think about where I'll be living. More like what I'll be doing."

Warren is quiet for a moment. Then: "I think about us. Where we'll be. Is that weird?"

"No." I pause. "I think about us, too."

"Oh yeah?" I can hear the smile in his voice. "About us being together?"

"Maybe," I tease, smiling, too.

His fingers dangle near my hand, then slowly thread their way through mine. "There was a full moon the first time we hung out."

"The night we had dinner with Lou and my dad?"

"Yvonne. You don't remember the first time we were alone together?"

I do, vaguely. It's just that Warren and I have spent so much time together in the last two years and it's so easy to be around him that it all sort of runs together. Like, being with him is just one big happy block in the schedule of my life.

"Was it that terrible party at Eugene's house?"

"Yeah, the night after your dad let him go. I don't think I've ever seen someone so drunk."

"You put him to bed! I remember thinking you were the nicest guy I'd ever been around."

He laughs. "Yeah, I'm a real saint."

"It was sweet." I squeeze his fingers. "All the guys I know would've let him keep drinking until he puked, just so they could laugh at him. Or drawn dicks on his face after he passed out."

Warren shrugs. "I was just doing what I would've wanted someone to do for me. He was a horrible server, but I felt bad that he lost his job."

We move off the path and lean against the fence that circles the reservoir. The moon is luminous, spider-webbed by tree branches that stretch to the sky.

"I can't believe we've known each other for two years," I say, looking away from the bright white disk.

"Feels like I've known you forever, Yvonne." His voice is soft, and then his hand is on my arm. I face him and when I look up, his smile is soft, too. "We may not know where we'll be in a year, but let's make it a good one until then, okay?"

I nod and then I put my arms around his neck and we kiss. He is hesitant at first, as if he's afraid my father is going to suddenly appear. I lean my body into Warren and he relaxes, his soft lips assured as they press against mine. As he remembers that it's just us right now, our only witness the moon.

3.

I meet Sabina at the set of concrete benches on the far side of the quad during lunch on Monday.

She's managed to snag our favorite seat, the bench under the giant eucalyptus. It's the coolest place to be out here on the unseasonably but predictably hot early-September days, and it's close enough to the tree that the thick, wide trunk can serve as a backrest. She scoots over to make room for me.

"So," Sabina says before I even sit down. "Damon has to have his party on Friday. His parents are going up to Tahoe for the weekend but sometimes they surprise him and come home early, so he doesn't want to risk having a bunch of people over on Saturday."

"Okay, but you know I have plans with Warren that night?" Friday is my birthday. I don't look at her as I slide onto the bench and drop my bag to the grass.

"Yeah, I know. I was just thinking you two could stop by if you get bored or whatever."

I pull out my lunch sack. "I'm pretty sure we're not going to get bored that night, Sabs."

I unwrap my peanut butter and banana sandwich, and, like every day, I'm glad Sabina is the only one around to watch me eat lunch. People think I get fancy lunches made and lovingly packed by my father the night before when the reality is that the more successful he becomes, the less time he has to cook for either of us. Lunches are out of the question.

"Is Warren too good to hang out with people still in high school or something?" Sabina always gets a bit defensive when she talks about Warren. She likes him well enough, but I think the idea of me dating someone older makes her feel left behind. Warren and I haven't slept together—yet—but I already crossed the great divide of best friendship when I had sex for the first time last year.

"He hangs out with me."

She rolls her eyes.

"Warren isn't big on parties." I take a bite and chew, watching Sabina pop open the plastic container she filled at the cafeteria's salad bar. "He barely goes out with the people he works with. He'd rather hang out one-on-one."

"I bet he would," she smirks, carefully drizzling lemon vinaigrette over her mixed greens.

Sabina Thompson is one of the only other black students at our private all-girls school in West Hollywood. We couldn't look more different. She has a gorgeous deep brown complexion, a tall figure with curves that I'd kill for, and natural hair that she usually wears in two French braids that trail down her back. I barely crest five feet and my skin is a honey brown and I keep my hair plaited in box braids thanks to the hair salon, because no one has ever taught me how to do anything else with it. Still, we didn't make it past the first day of sixth grade before one of the teachers confused us. I think both of us knew it wouldn't be the last time, and we became fast friends by the end of our first week at Courtland Academy.

I take a drink from my bottle of apple juice. "He wants to make dinner for me. That's nice."

"Yeah, yeah, it's great, but you should still stop by if you can." She looks at me sideways. "You can't leave me alone with Dame and all his weirdo friends."

"Hey! I slept with one of those weirdo friends."

She raises her eyebrows. "Exactly. What if I mirror your poor judgment?"

"Poor judgment? Cody is a straight-A honor student and president of his class. And objectively hot, in case you've forgotten."

"Fine. That was an unsuccessful guilt trip." She sighs. "I just want to celebrate with you, but I guess Saturday will have to do. It's a big deal, Yvonne. *Eighteen*."

"Well, if I see you on Saturday that means I'll have the best birthday weekend ever, because I'll get to see my two favorite people." I bump her shoulder with mine and take a large bite of my sandwich.

She smiles in spite of herself, sips from her bottle of water, and looks at me. Her voice is noticeably softer as she asks, "Have you heard anything from her?"

"No." I don't look up.

Sabina and I stopped saying my mother's name a long time ago, which is better than my father and I, who never mention her at all.

"I just thought maybe since this is your eighteenth—"

"She didn't do anything for thirteen or sixteen or any other year. Why start now?" I don't bother making my voice lighter or forcing my lips into a wry smile. Not with Sabina. "She's probably out somewhere celebrating that she can officially cut ties with me forever and not get called out on it."

"I'm sorry, girl."

"Yeah." I set down my sandwich. I slathered on too much peanut butter this morning. The ratio of bread to bananas is totally off, and my tongue feels like it will permanently stick to the roof of my mouth if I keep eating. "Me too, Sabs."

After school, I head to the music room, violin case strapped over my shoulder. I've been toting it around since I first started playing in the school orchestra, in fifth grade, the year before I got to Courtland Academy. I thought that after carrying it around for so long, it would start to feel like a part of me, like the violin had grown into an impermanent limb that I no longer noticed. But the truth is that I've gotten so used to having it with me it feels almost like a friend. I'd feel naked walking through the hallways without it.

Ms. Ortiz looks up from her podium and smiles when I walk in. The room is large, filled with dozens of music stands, a piano, various types of percussion instruments, a couple of cellos and a bass, and filing cabinets stuffed with sheet music. Somehow Ms. Ortiz keeps it in immaculate condition, and we all like her enough to help out with that.

"Thanks for stopping by, Yvonne."

I start to sit, but she gestures toward my instrument. "I was actually wondering if you could play for me."

I stare at her. "Right now?"

"Please."

"But I'm not warmed up...."

"I'll let it slide." She points to a music stand next to her podium, and when I move to look at it, I see a familiar piece of sheet music. It's a movement from a Vivaldi concerto.

"We played this last year," I say, stalling for time. It's one thing to be surrounded by the other students in class, but I feel shy standing here alone in front of Ortiz. Exposed.

"I know," Ortiz responds. She doesn't have a desk in here, so she sits down in one of the front-row chairs.

I slowly remove my bow and instrument from the case, trying to remember the last time I played this. I practiced with Denis until I could execute it to his liking, but I could tell he thought it took me too long to do so.

I say a silent prayer to my violin before I begin to play. I never used to do that, not until the last year or so, when I could see the frustration in Denis. He was always frustrated, and at first I couldn't tell if that was simply his personality or me misreading his strong French accent. But it wasn't long before the life in his eyes faded more and more each time we met for lessons, and I could practically see him twitching with impatience as I played.

I try to put all of that out of my mind as I touch my bow down on the strings. The piece is lively and quick, the type of music that would accompany impish elves in a fairy-tale scene of a ballet. I used to feel so alive as I played it, my mood shifting to match the piece. But I am mechanical as I work through the movement, and though I'm trying to impress Ortiz, my intonation is off. My heart isn't in the piece, and it makes me feel like my violin and I are working against each other instead of together.

Ortiz holds up her hand and I stop, grateful.

"Am I in trouble?" I ask, only half joking. Anyone who's had class with Ms. Ortiz loves her, but she's not afraid to tell you how it is. She expects a lot out of her students, which puts us all a little on edge.

"I don't think you've ever been in trouble a day in your life, Yvonne."

I'm no bastion of obedience, but it's easy to be good around Ortiz.

She pats the chair next to her, and I swiftly slip my violin back into its case before I join her.

Ortiz squints her warm brown eyes at me. "How do you feel about what you just played?"

"Okay, I guess. I mean, it wasn't perfect. My intonation—"

"I'm not talking about the technical part. How did you *feel*?"

I shrug. I didn't feel much of anything, besides a little embarrassed and wholly unprepared. And I don't know how to admit that to the woman who is always saying that we have to feel the music from inside.

"Yvonne, you've been different this year. We've only been back in school a few weeks, but you're not your usual self. Is there anything you want to talk about?"

I thought I would have worked up the courage to tell

Ortiz that Denis decided to stop working with me this summer, but I never did. Now I'm sitting here wishing I could curl up into a pea-size ball and roll right out of this room.

"I'm not taking lessons with Denis anymore."

"Oh." She pauses, which makes me think she knows the answer to the question she's about to ask. "You've started working with someone new?"

"I'm not working with anyone, Ms. Ortiz. Denis dropped me, and I didn't think anyone else would want to take me on, so…" I look down at my hands, thinking about the day he told me he no longer had room for me on his roster.

"I'm sorry to hear that, Yvonne."

She doesn't ask why, so she must know the answer to that, as well. I look up at her. "Am I really that bad? Honestly?"

Ms. Ortiz sighs. "It's not about good or bad for me. You used to have a spark in your eyes when you played."

I don't know whether to feel better about how up-front Denis was with his feelings, even though his words made me cry—"It is simply not worth my time to continue with someone who is not improving"—or how Ortiz is trying to preserve my feelings but isn't really answering my question.

"What happened?" she presses, her voice gentle.

"I don't know.…I guess I just stopped loving it. I don't get excited by the pieces anymore. Maybe a few here and there, but it's all sort of boring. Uninspiring. No offense," I say, looking at her from the corner of my eye.

"I'm sure Mozart and Beethoven will forgive you," she teases. "Was it something Denis did? Or me?"

I shake my head.

"You can be honest."

"No, really, Ms. Ortiz. I can't look back at one day when I wanted to stop playing. I guess it just got less exciting over time."

She nods slowly. "That happens. When we spoke in the spring, you were thinking about conservatories...."

I was thinking about them and talking about them, but I knew I wasn't at the level of most of the applicants. I certainly wasn't a prodigy, one of the kids who have to complete their schoolwork through tutors because they've been busy traveling the world for competitions and performing with world-famous orchestras since they were ten years old.

Denis said that if I worked very hard and focused on music 200 percent, he could get me to a place where I would feel okay about auditioning. *Okay*, not *good*. As soon as he said that, I realized I wasn't up to the challenge. You need raw talent or supernatural determination to make it to that level—usually both. Even if someone was gracious enough to suggest that I possessed a bit of both attributes, I knew it wasn't enough to succeed. And that made me feel shameful. Lazy. Like I've been wasting everyone's time, including my own.

"Conservatories are not on my list," I say.

Not that there's an actual list. Every time I start to look at college websites, I get too overwhelmed by all the questions in my head: *What will I study? Where will I go? Do I stay close to home to be near my father, even though we're basically strangers? If I go far away, will our relationship become even more distant? What will happen with Warren and me?* There's always so much to think about that I end up clicking out of the websites and watching videos instead.

"Normally I'd suggest applying to schools with a music program, where you can study other subjects that interest you and still have violin." Ortiz pauses again. "But those require passion and drive, too. They'd expect you to take those classes seriously, and I'm not sure I could write a letter of recommendation knowing your heart isn't in it."

"I'll figure it out," I say quickly, but I'm not fooling either one of us. Gradually losing my love for playing was bad enough, but realizing my talent alone can't save me is demoralizing. Having no idea what I'm going to do is downright scary.

"For what it's worth, Yvonne, I still believe you to be a good musician. No one is disputing that," Ortiz says after a long pause between us. "But you have to want it more than anything else in this world to give your life to it. And sometimes even that isn't enough."

I take a deep breath. I wanted to study music in college. I wanted to play violin professionally because it's comfortable—and, really, because I don't know how to do anything else.

Denis's words hurt, but they weren't a surprise. Hearing Ortiz say I just don't want it, that my issues stem from an emotional place, is more of a gut punch. I can practice until my fingers bleed, but I can't control my emotions.

"It feels like I've wasted the last eleven years of my life," I say, thinking back to that initial trip to the violin store and to my first lesson with Denis after that.

Ortiz gives me a sad smile. "It's not a waste. This isn't as dire as it sounds. You never know where you'll end up." She squeezes my shoulder as we walk to the door.

I step out into the hallway and look back at her. "Thanks. For the honesty."

"Thanks to you. For not making me feel bad about being honest." She leans against the doorframe. "And, Yvonne, you know, you can always have music. Just because it's not at the center of your life, that doesn't mean you can't have it at all."

4.

When I was younger, my father would work the breakfast and lunch shifts at the restaurant where he was a line cook so he could get off in time to pick me up from school. Then, when I started at Courtland, he became sous chef for his mentor, Lou, whose upscale restaurant was only open for dinner. Large, white-haired Lou liked having me around, so it wasn't a problem to go there after school while my father worked. If the restaurant wasn't busy, I could sit at a high-top table in the corner of the bar area and do my homework, sipping on Shirley Temples that Lou would bring over himself. On the nights when the wait was long enough that the bar filled with people killing time, I would sit alone in Lou's tiny office and my father would come back and check on me every once in a while, sweat glistening on his forehead as he slid a plate of whatever they were serving in front of me.

It never occurred to me that I had developed a good palate until I started talking to Sabina about the food I'd eat during the week. Things she'd never had, like bone marrow and steak tartare and grilled ramps, which tasted like a head of garlic and an onion had a baby and made my breath smell the next day. I was so used to eating whatever Dad put in front of me, and I guess because of that I've never been picky.

Nobody had to tell me I wouldn't see much of my father when he opened his own restaurant. He was still working for Lou, and every minute he wasn't there was spent crafting his own business plan. Sometimes the smell of his late-night smoking sessions would waft under the door of the sunroom and into my bedroom, waking me at odd hours of the morning. And sometimes I would go out and sit with him, enduring the stench for a chance to tell him about my day or ask him for something I needed at school or for violin.

I always feel a little out of place at his restaurant and it still surprises me. Maybe it's because there's no Lou to bring me grenadine-laced ginger ale. Maybe it's because I've never sat in my father's office chair doing math problems while I waited for him to bring back a plate of food. Or maybe it's simply because I don't know my father that well. It's always baffled me how critics who've never even met him can write about the restaurant with such authority, theorizing about his motivations behind certain dishes.

I promised Sabina a free dinner if she met me here tonight, but she has to eat with her parents. Sabina's moms aren't as lax about child-rearing as my dad is—they definitely don't know about his love for greenery—and they believe in meals with everyone at the table during the week. But they know me and love me, and they usually say yes when she wants to hang out with me instead. I think they feel bad about how much my father works.

When I knock on the glass of the front door, Warren is the one to come get me. We just saw each other yesterday, but something flutters in my chest when his eyes light on my face. We smile at each other.

"Hey." He gives me a quick hug as I step inside, though I get the feeling, like always, that he wants to kiss me, too. He reaches around me to lock the door, then says, "You just missed family meal, but I could whip up something for you real quick?"

Whatever they ate smells incredible. The peanut butter and banana sandwich only filled me up for a couple of hours; my stomach was grumbling even before I went to talk to Ortiz. But I shake my head. "You should save your energy for my birthday dinner. Five courses, right?"

"Eight," he says, not breaking into a grin until I do. "You sure?"

"Yeah, I'm fine. I'm not staying. I just need to talk to him."

"Before you do—I got some good news," he says, his smile turning sheepish. "*SoCal Weekly* wants to interview me."

"What?" I smile at him so hard I'm sure my face will split in two. "That's fucking amazing, War!"

"Thanks." Then he looks down at his feet and I'm staring at the top of his light-brown head. Most people think Warren is white because of his light skin and his hair that hardly holds a curl, but he identifies as black. His dad is white, but Warren was raised by his mom and only knows her side of the family.

I tilt my head at him. "It *is* amazing, right? *SoCal Weekly* is a big deal."

He shrugs. "I mean, yeah it is. Of course it is. I just don't want them to wish they'd picked someone else. I've never been interviewed before. What if my answers are awful?"

"You'll be great," I say. "Just pretend that you're talking to me."

He steps closer and gives me a lazy grin. "So I should tell the reporter how much I want to kiss her right now?"

"She might even say yes, if her father weren't standing in the back of the room."

"Right." Warren briefly touches my fingertips with his, making my breath catch. "Let me take you back there. Careful, though. He's in a mood. There was an incident at the butcher's."

"Got it."

My father is pretty chill in general, but he's been known to go off on a hot-tempered tirade when something goes wrong at the restaurant. He spends a lot of time making sure things run smoothly, so he doesn't like it when other people fuck up. He's not so hard on me, but before I started at Courtland's upper school, he said he wanted me to remember three things:

1. To use protection if I was going to have sex,
2. To never drive if I was going to drink, and
3. To never forget that I had to work twice as hard as white people to get half of what they did.

Warren walks me to the back and I find myself leaning closer to him, inadvertently searching for that clean, soapy smell that lingers on his skin until he really gets going in the kitchen. I wave at the hostess and a couple of servers I know as we make our way to the rear of the restaurant. Warren leaves me by the entrance of the kitchen and walks across the room, clapping my father on the back to let him know I'm here. Dad looks up and if he's surprised to see me, it doesn't show. He holds up his index finger—he has to finish talking to one of the cooks. Warren looks back at me and smiles before he disappears into his work. The flutters start again and I wonder about my birthday dinner—if that will be the night we're finally together.

"Tell me nothing bad's happened," Dad says when he's standing in front of me a couple of minutes later. He doesn't sound as irritable as I expected. Just tired. It seems too early for him to sound so weary, considering they haven't yet opened for the evening.

"What?"

"Yvonne, you're here. You're never here. Is everything all right?"

"Oh. Yeah. I just need to tell you something. I didn't want to wait up."

His face relaxes and he motions for me to follow him to his office, which is just as tiny as Lou's but not as cluttered. He doesn't like too much stuff sitting around. "What's up?"

I take a seat in the chair against the far wall, but he leans on the edge of his desk, clearly not wanting this to take too long.

"I talked to Ms. Ortiz and... I don't know what to do."

He frowns, his thick eyebrows furrowed. He's a big guy, tall and solid, with a receding hairline that he tries to hide by shaving his brown head bald. "Ms. Ortiz...?"

"Dad. My orchestra teacher."

"Sorry. I always think of Denis with you and violin."

"Not anymore."

"Right. So, what did Ms. Ortiz have to say?"

"She wants me to consider other programs besides music. She says the passion isn't coming through...and I'm not good enough to coast on my talent."

"Come on now. You're great. I've been listening to you play for years. I always thought that Denis was an entitled asshole."

My father's not wrong about Denis, but I have to defend what he and Ortiz said. They both can't be wrong. But most of all, I know in my heart that applying to conservatories was a false dream. I wanted to go because violin is the only thing I know how to do, not because I love it like I used to.

"I'd have to practice almost nonstop to be good enough to even audition for conservatories. And...I don't want it enough. I've always liked playing the violin...but maybe I've outgrown it."

"Ah." He scratches the side of his head. "I thought you loved that thing. Sure paid enough for the one you have now."

"I know." I sigh. "I did love it. I still do sometimes...just not enough. And now I don't know if I should quit orchestra or finish out the year. What's the point of being there every day if I'm just going to stop once I graduate?"

"We can find you something else," he says quickly, and I'm instantly reminded of all the lessons and activities that didn't take when I was younger. How relieved he seemed when the violin stuck and I'd finally found my thing.

I was relieved, too. I didn't understand how some of my

friends found such joy participating in multiple activities when I had so much trouble finding one thing that excited me. It wasn't just about playing, though. My violin started to feel like a companion. When I'm lonely, I always have my music. The thought of leaving that behind scares me almost more than having no other options.

"I'm not sure there's anything else I want to do."

He pauses, and I can tell that he's thinking carefully about what he's going to say. "Well, after graduation...you could always work here for a while if you needed to."

"Here?"

He raises an eyebrow.

"No, I mean, it's great here. But what would I do?"

My father shrugs. "We'd figure something out."

"Really?"

"You're my only child, Yvonne." His eyes fall to the floor before they move back up to meet mine. "It's not in my interest to see you fail. And you're young. College will still be there when you figure out what to do. You've got time."

"You already knew you wanted to be a chef when you were my age." And knowing my father had it all figured out by eighteen makes me feel like I've already failed. If he and Warren both realized this was their calling, why is it so hard for me to find mine?

"Don't give me so much credit. I was a fuckup for a good long while before I got my shit together." Dad laughs at my shocked expression, which makes me smile. His laughter is infrequent but always welcome. "What? You knew that."

I slide my hands over the front pocket of the leather backpack in my lap. "Yeah, but you don't really talk about it now that you have all this."

"I don't believe in dwelling on past regrets. I wouldn't be the same person without them." He gives me his best attempt at a smile, but his mind is already back on the problems he has to deal with here. "Anything else before I go back out there? You want to stay for dinner?"

I look around his office, at how clinical it is compared with the coziness of Lou's. It feels like a doctor's office, filled only with necessary objects, and there's nothing on display that proves he has a life outside of this place. He hasn't changed the photo of me that sits on his desk in years. My braces-filled seventh-grade smile peeks out from the picture frame sitting crookedly next to his keyboard. I don't know him any better now than I did then.

"No, I'm not that hungry. Thanks."

"Let me send you home with something, then."

I leave a few minutes later with a hot dinner slipped inside a sturdy paper bag. Warren sneaks away to walk me out.

"Glad I got to see you," he says, his hand lingering on my arm.

My skin tingles with goose bumps. I look at him and smile. "Me too."

He pulls me to the side, away from the front door, and presses his lips to mine. One of his hands rests on my waist, the other cupping one side of my face. I kiss him back, losing myself in the warmth of his mouth on mine, and I don't realize I've dropped the paper bag I was holding until I hear it thunk on the sidewalk.

I pull away and laugh, burying my face in his shoulder. Warren grins and picks up the bag, pecking me on the cheek before he hands it back to me.

I squeeze his hand, then get in my car and drive home to eat supper alone.

5.

I try not to let it get to me, but the talk with Ortiz stings.

I think about it every time I pick up my violin, which is every day, because I don't want to quit orchestra. Not yet. Even though guilt seeps into my fingers every time I unpack my instrument and pick up my bow. It feels like I'm betraying a friend when I think of giving up the violin. I know our relationship has changed, but it's hard not to feel sad about it when it's always been there for me.

It seems silly, but I feel like it knows what I'm thinking. The notes sound distorted. False. For now, I can blend in with the rest of the orchestra; we've just started learning a new piece for the holiday program, so it's easy enough to brush off any sour notes. But my focus isn't there. And I avoid looking at Ortiz because it reminds me that she's known how detached I've been . . . maybe before I realized it myself.

By the time the Wednesday before my birthday rolls around, I feel restless. Too full of extra energy I can't burn off. I don't know if it's the anticipation of my Friday night with Warren or the new but very real anxiety of not knowing what I'm going to do with my life. Or maybe it's just a precursor to the knot that plants itself in my stomach every year at this time when I wonder if my mother will acknowledge my existence.

Locking myself in my room with my violin used to help, but now . . .

I slide up next to Sabina's locker after the last bell. She's already there, grabbing a couple of books to stick in her bag. "I'm going with Damon to get alcohol for the party. Come with?"

"He's going to use his fake to buy all that booze?"

Neither Sabina nor I have fake IDs. I've never needed to, not with Warren willing to do pretty much anything I ask. Sabina's too worried about getting caught. She worries a lot, mostly about letting down her moms. They don't put a ton of outward pressure on her, but they are so put together and so seemingly perfect that even I feel intimidated when I'm around them.

"No, his older brother is going, too. We have to meet him over at USC." She rolls her eyes.

"Now?"

"Yeah, why?" She slams her locker shut and adjusts the bag on her shoulder.

I strap on my violin case and we start walking out to the parking lot, weaving through the steadily thinning hallway as people make their way to practices and club meetings and outside, like us, to escape for the rest of the day.

"I'm going to Venice. Thought you might want to come." I shrug, trying to look totally nonchalant, as if Venice is somewhere I go often. Or somewhere she'd want to accompany me.

"Venice. Like, Venice *Beach*?" Sabina makes a terrible face, as if I've suggested we go hang out in Skid Row for a few hours.

"Come on, it's not that bad."

"It's dirty. And it always smells like a vat of patchouli exploded. Why are you going there?"

I shrug. "I don't know. The beach sounds nice sometimes, I guess."

She looks at me and puts her palm over my forehead as we walk out into the sunshine. "Seriously, are you sick or something? You wouldn't even go to Santa Monica for McKenzie's birthday."

"That doesn't count," I say, ducking away from her hand. "I had cramps. And anyway, Santa Monica is so different. It's so—"

"Clean? Not scary?"

"*Polished.*"

Sabina gives me the side eye as we approach her car. "Agree to disagree. But, really. What's in Venice?"

"A guy."

A strange look passes over her face. Not quite judgment, but something like it. "Don't you have a date with Warren on Friday?"

I do. And it's technically our first, since he's always been wary of us officially going out before I turn eighteen. It's the same reason he always stops us before we have sex. Warren and I have both known plenty of people who dated older in high school, and it's not like my father would press charges or something. But my age has always made Warren nervous. Like he's taking advantage of me. It took a whole year for him to kiss me.

"It's not like that with him...the beach guy," I say, though when I think of listening and watching him play, I'm not sure my feelings match my words. "He's a musician. He performs with a girl, and he plays the violin."

Sabina unlocks her car, tosses her bag into the back seat, and turns to face me. "Street performers?"

"Don't say it like that. They're actual musicians, you know."

"What's so special about them?"

"I guess that's what I'm going back to find out. They're

really talented, and they looked so *happy*, and they weren't even playing classical music. Maybe some of their magic can rub off on me."

"Fair enough," she says, because Sabina has listened to me wrestle with my feelings over violin for a while now. After Denis dropped me and then after my talk with Ortiz. "Well, I'll come down and pick you up if you get mugged, I guess."

"Ha ha. Have fun with Dame."

"It's sure to be a blast," she says drily, getting into the driver's seat.

The beach is decidedly cooler today than when I was here a couple of weeks ago. I wrap my arms tightly around myself, wishing I'd thought to bring a sweater. That's one reason I could probably never live on the Westside, especially at one of the beaches. It's so much cooler by the water, sometimes a twenty-degree difference compared with where we live on the Eastside.

I walk right to the spot where the guy was the last time, not bothering to pretend I'm here for anything else. I wish there was some meaningful scene, like I heard his music straining through the crowd as soon as I hit the boardwalk and followed it all the way to where he was set up on the sand, a beatific smile on his face as he played.

But he's not playing, and there's no *him* at all. The girl is here, perched on a folding chair with her viola resting carefully on her lap and her phone in her hand. Beside her, the other chair is occupied by a violin, but its owner is nowhere to be found.

I shift from foot to foot for a moment, unsure if I should stay and wait until they start playing again or walk away before she sees me.

Too late.

She looks up and back to her phone but then makes eye contact with me again. She doesn't look away this time, and there's no one to hide behind because of course if they're not playing, there's no crowd standing here.

She raises an eyebrow when I don't say anything. "Yeah?"

"Um." I don't know why I'm so tongue-tied whenever I'm here, but it's as if my mouth has completely forgotten how to work.

She sighs. "Looking for Omar?"

Omar.

Before I can respond, footsteps scuffle through the sand-covered sidewalk and the guy—seriously, is he her brother or boyfriend?—is standing next to me. "Who's looking for me?"

The girl shrugs. "Her, I guess," she says before staring back at the phone in her palm.

"Oh. Hey." Then he looks at me a little closer. "I've seen you here before."

"Yeah, I . . ." I hope he doesn't remember how awkward

I was last time, but he can't, right? He's on Venice Beach, a place constantly teeming with tourists and locals who are always doing or saying the wrong thing. I couldn't stick out to him more than anyone else.

"Well, now you know my name, so it's probably only fair if I know yours, too," he says easily, like this happens all the time, girls coming up to look for him on the beach.

I hope not.

Standing this close, I see that some of his dark brown locs are streaked with gold, intermittently bleached by the sun.

"Yvonne," I blurt, relieved to finally know what to say.

"Cool to meet you." He nods behind him. "That's Keely." She doesn't look up.

"So ..." His eyes are friendly but curious.

"I play, too," I say quietly. "Violin."

"No shit?" The smile that breaks out takes over his whole face, and it makes me relax. A little bit.

"No shit." I smile back.

"You come down here to give us some tips?" He's still grinning, though.

"God, no. I just..." I pause, trying to think of a good reason to explain why I'm here, but decide the truth is probably best. If I leave here embarrassed, I won't ever have to see him again. "I'm actually having a hard time with violin right now. I play in my school's orchestra, and I haven't felt much of anything for it lately. But then I came here and saw you two and...I just really like your style."

I've always felt a special connection to people who play the same instrument as me, and it feels the same with Omar—but stronger. His understanding eyes and relaxed demeanor don't hurt, but there's something more here. For the first time in a while, I feel excited to be talking about music. It's like he's flipped on a switch to a light that's been darkened so long I forgot it existed.

Keely clears her throat, a sound that manages to cut through all the peripheral noise of the crowds and the softly crashing waves of the ocean and land right in my ear. "O, it's time."

"Gimme a sec," he says over his shoulder. Then, to me: "Listen, I have to get back to work, but if you want to talk sometime, I know a little about that orchestra life. And how stifling it can be. I went to Berklee."

"Oh, up north?"

"No." He smiles as if he's used to my response, and as soon as he does, I want to kick myself. "The one in Boston."

Of course he didn't mean UC Berkeley.

"I know it," I say, my face flushing hot. "My teacher went there."

"Cool. Well, if you ever want to talk—"

"*Omar.*" Behind him, Keely is done with her phone, her

viola propped up vertically on her knees, guarding her like a shield.

He doesn't bother turning around this time, just shoots me an apologetic look. "Give me your phone and I'll put my number in."

I do and he does, and Keely glares at his back the whole time. She can't be his girlfriend, but maybe an ex? The way she's looking at me, I know she'd rather never see me again. I watch Omar key in his number instead.

"Call me," he says with a grin before he heads back to his violin and his impatient partner. "Anytime, Yvonne."

"Thank you." My skin burns hot when I realize I'm already wondering how long I should wait to get in touch with him. I tell myself it's about the violin . . . but if it was just about music, I wouldn't be so nervous. "That's really nice."

I walk away before they start playing, but not before I hear Keely saying, "What the fuck was that about?"

6.

I **don't feel any different when I open my eyes the**
morning of my eighteenth birthday.

After my shower, I stand in front of the bathroom mirror
for a while. I don't look any different, either. I think about
how Warren and I are probably going to take the next step
tonight and breathe in deeply. It was easier to imagine being
with him when it was a far-off possibility or maybe something that would never happen. I used to think he was using
my age as an excuse, that he wasn't really interested and
didn't know how to tell me. But I don't think you can fake
the way you look at someone you really like—Warren Engel
can't, anyway.

Dad is still asleep when I leave for school, but there's a card on the kitchen table. I put it in my bag to read later. My father gets too flustered when he tries to buy personalized gifts, but he's consistently generous with the birthday cash. Warren texts when I'm getting into my car and says he can't wait to see me later, that he's got everything planned out for dinner.

At school, Sabina has decorated my locker with multi-colored party streamers and balloons and a HAPPY BIRTHDAY sign made from poster board that people have started to write messages on. She sets a flower crown made of real pink roses atop my head and says I have to wear it all day. Lunch is two trays overflowing with curly fries from the caf and strawberry cupcakes that Sabina made last night.

"It's funny how everyone's nice to you on your birthday," I say, resting my back against our favorite bench in the quad as I stretch my legs out on the grass.

"Why wouldn't they be?" Beside me, Sabina methodically licks buttercream frosting from the top of a cupcake.

"No, I mean, it's cool, but it's, like, one day a year when pretty much everyone agrees not to be an asshole to someone. Or if they *are* a dick and find out it's your birthday, then they're all sorry, like it makes a difference."

"Has someone been a dick to you today?"

"I think everyone is aware it's my birthday today," I say, touching the crown on my head. "Thanks. Really. It's nice."

"If your best friend doesn't make your day special, who will?" Sabina polishes off the rest of her cupcake.

"Warren," I say with a straight face.

She watches me while she finishes chewing, her eyes narrowed. "You're lucky it's your birthday," she says after washing down the cupcake with a sip of water.

"Why?"

She brushes crumbs from her hands and gives me a toothy grin. "Because I just stopped myself from being a dick to you."

Warren tells me to come over at seven, but when I get to his apartment, he's not there.

I knock four times before I use the spare key he gave me and let myself in. He's probably out buying some last-minute thing for the meal. For someone who works so closely with food, Warren is terrible at grocery shopping. He's always forgetting something on his list or forgetting his list entirely and having to shop by memory because he refuses to save things on his phone like a normal person.

As usual, Warren's place is unbearably tidy. His favorite issues of *Food & Wine* are stacked on the counter that divides the galley kitchen from the rest of his studio apartment. Even the bed shoved into the opposite corner of the room is made.

I look in the fridge to see if I can tell what he's making. My eyes immediately light on the pink box on the bottom shelf. A bakery box. I didn't tell him I wanted a cake, but of course he wouldn't have made it himself. Warren says baking doesn't make sense, that there are too many rules; I like the mandatory precision it requires. I should wait to open the box, but I peek inside. The cake is gorgeous. Dark-chocolate ganache with two chocolate rosettes in the corner and HAPPY BIRTH-DAY YVONNE swirled in perfect white script in the center.

I consider taking a picture to show Sabina how thoughtful he is, but I don't want her to think I didn't appreciate her cupcakes. I look at it for a few more seconds before I close the lid, wondering if it's too pretty to eat.

I text Warren to tell him I'm here, then plop down on the futon. I've never been so comfortable at someone else's place. Not even Sabina's, where I've been going since I was twelve. Sabina is always cool, of course, but I worry about doing or saying the wrong thing in front of her moms. I don't really know what it's like to have another parent besides my dad, but I know how we are with each other isn't so conventional. We talk to each other more like distant roommates than father and daughter, so I get self-conscious when I'm around other parents.

I guess I knew there was something different about Warren not long after we met. And it didn't take long to feel like I'd known him forever. I told him about my mom only a few weeks after we started hanging out. Some people I've been going to school with for years don't know anything about her except that she's not around.

I told him how all my memories of her are happy. How we

used to go everywhere together, and that lots of those places weren't kid appropriate. There were concerts and expensive lunches in Beverly Hills and hiking trails that were so steep in some places, she had to carry me on her back. I told him how I hate that I have just a couple of blurry pictures of her: a profile shot where she's wearing giant sunglasses and sitting on a stoop that's not ours, and a faraway photo of her in front of the Pantages Theatre, waving at the person behind the camera. I don't remember much about what she looked like—only her brown skin, the same warm shade as mine, and her black hair that was always big and soft.

Maybe it's because his dad left, too, but Warren didn't flinch when I said everything was perfect until the day she left. That I had no clue she was unhappy. I guess maybe I sensed there was something off with her and Dad. She spent more time with me than him, and he spent all his time at work. But I was six years old. It's been twelve years now and I still barely understand how someone can say they love you to the moon and back one day and then disappear forever.

My phone rings. I don't have to look down to know that it's Warren. And I think maybe it's a bad sign that he's calling and not texting, because my heart starts to beat in that nervous way that tells me something's wrong, no matter how much I don't want it to be.

"I'm so sorry," he says as soon as I answer. "I got caught up here at the restaurant and . . . I haven't left yet."

I try to keep my voice calm. "Why are you at the restaurant? Did he tell you to come in?"

On my birthday?

Warren sighs. "Jameson called in and I told your dad I could stop by for a couple of hours. Just to help him get things running, and then I'd have to leave."

"But you let him talk you into staying."

"I'm so sorry, Yvonne." In the background, I hear my father's voice over the usual kitchen sounds of clinking plates and hissing skillets. "I have everything ready at home. As soon as I get there, I'll start on the food, okay?"

"Did you not tell him we have plans?" Not only is my voice no longer calm, it's pitching higher and higher each time I speak. I put my hand to my throat as if I can will it to sound different.

"I'm his sous chef now." He pauses. "I need to be here for him. You know how this stuff goes—"

"And *you* know I can't be alone on my birthday. Why make this big deal about cooking me dinner and it being our first date if—this is really shitty, Warren."

He sighs again. "Please don't be mad. I'm sorry. I—"

"If you're really sorry, you'll walk out of there right now." My hand is shaking and the phone is shaking and I think my voice might be, too.

"Yvonne, please."

That means he's staying. I don't say anything, just let the silence grow between us.

"Yvonne. I can't choose between you and my job."

"I think you just did." I hang up before he can finish pleading.

Warren has never disappointed me like this, and maybe it isn't fair to put that sort of expectation on anyone, but I thought I was safe with him. And he knows how hard my birthday is each year—trying to balance the foolish hope that I'll hear from my mother with the reality that I know I never will. I believed him when he said he'd never felt about anyone the way he feels about me. I thought I could let my guard down.

Before I leave, I take the pink box from the fridge, carefully remove the cake, and smash the whole beautiful thing on the kitchen floor.

7.

Damon lives a couple of streets over from Sabina—close enough to walk from her house but far enough away that her parents won't hear the party. I circle the block a few times looking for parking without any luck.

When I do find a spot, just as someone is pulling away from the curb, I parallel park on the first try. Then I shut off the ignition and sit. I feel numb.

I think about going inside for a while. After ten minutes have passed, I know I won't be able to handle it. I'm angry with Warren, but I'm more disappointed in myself for trusting him. Maybe I should have come to the party with Sabina all along. Except now I'm here, and I don't want to go in.

I could drive away. Let Sabina celebrate with me tomorrow,

like we planned; a day late yet no less appreciated. But I know I'll feel better if I see her, if only for a few minutes. I text her.

> Parked outside. Please come out.

Her reply shows up almost instantly.

> Just come in! Not too many people yet. Dame already wasted of course

> Can't

A couple of minutes later she's running toward my car. I see her pounding down the sidewalk in my rearview mirror and then, before I can click the locks, she's rapping at my passenger side window with her knuckles, shout-whispering at me to let her in.

She slides into the seat, takes one look at my face, and wraps her arms tight around my shoulders. "You okay?"

I shake my head, so she keeps hugging me. She smells like beer and cigarettes. She only smokes when she's around Damon.

"Warren stood me up," I say when I finally pull away.

"What? Oh, *that* mother—" she starts, her eyes narrowing into angry slits that I'm happy aren't meant for me.

"No, I mean, he called. But he's at the restaurant. He's

not even supposed to be working tonight." I inhale, then let out the breath long and slow. "I really wanted tonight to happen, Sabs."

"Your first date?"

"Yeah, and being *together*. Finally."

"He's an idiot. Who wants to be cooped up in a hot-ass kitchen when they could be having dinner with hot-ass you?"

I smile just a little.

"Really. You look superhot, Yvonne."

I'm wearing a dress that I've been saving. It's lacy and cornflower blue with long sleeves and a short skirt with a scalloped hem. "It's not too much?"

"It's amazing. And now dumb Warren won't even get to see you in it." She reaches for my hand. "Want to come in and show it off? Everyone's been asking about you."

"I don't think so, Sabs." The thought of seeing anyone but my best friend right now makes me feel a little sick, honestly. "You know it's not really about him. Not totally. It's..."

"Her."

"Yeah. I *still* thought I might hear from her this year. What if I never get over it? I just want a normal birthday."

Sabina squeezes my hand. "Want me to come over? We can stop by my house and grab some pajamas and snacks. Or you can stay over if you want. Mom and Mama Jess are out on date night."

"No, I just need to go home, I think."

"Alone?"

I nod. "I'll call you if I change my mind."

"If you're sure."

"Positive."

She hugs me again. "Happy birthday. I love you."

"I love you, too, Sabs."

When I get home, I try to lie down, but I'm too angry to sleep.

I keep thinking about that cake. Warren fucked up, but the cake is the one thing he got right. My dad doesn't bake, and I don't think it ever occurred to him that I'd want a cake without a birthday party, which I've never asked for since my mother left. Cakes were her area. The night before my birthday she'd tuck me in like normal, but then I'd hear her banging around in the kitchen. Sometimes I'd fall asleep before she put it in to bake, and the sweet smell from the oven would wake me, tempting me to go out and ask for a piece. I never did, though. She always looked so happy to present it to me in the morning, and it's the one time of year she encouraged me to eat cake for breakfast.

I don't know the recipe by heart, and for a few moments, I consider trying something totally different. If not, I'll have to drag out my mother's old recipe box, the one with index cards of her favorite baked goods scrawled in handwriting I haven't seen in years. This isn't the night to go down memory lane.

But if I want it to be accurate, I'll need to look. And I don't want anyone else's cake. I want the one that I used to wake up to, the one that proves there was a time my mother loved me.

I go to the kitchen and find the card right away and place it on the counter, making sure I have everything I need. I run my fingers over the faded ink and spots of dried cake batter that have stuck to the card. I think maybe it will make me feel closer to her, more forgiving of the fact that my birthday is almost officially over and for yet another year, she's absent.

It just makes me angrier.

I lose myself in the task of baking. I measure dry ingredients, cream butter and eggs, and melt squares of unsweetened chocolate over the double broiler. I pour the batter into my mother's old cake pans, which have been sitting unused at the back of the cabinet for so long that they're practically antiques. It's always strange touching her things, remembering that she was once here, living and breathing in the same house as my father and me. A few minutes after I slide it into the oven, the cake makes the kitchen—the whole house, maybe—smell impossibly sweet and delicious.

After the layers have cooled, I move them to the heavy glass cake stand and take way too long frosting them. I want it to look perfect. It's only yellow cake, nothing fancy. But it feels good to have done something for myself instead of moping about all the ways I've been disappointed today. It's a better way to end my birthday, rather than being actively angry at two people who've proven they don't care enough about me.

I remember getting into bed but not falling asleep, and when I open my eyes, Warren is gently shaking my shoulder.

"Hey." He gives me a nervous smile.

I look at him for several silent moments as I wake up. For a few seconds, I think I'm at his house, asleep on the futon. But no, I'm in my bedroom, and I'm still wearing my dress, and the clock on my wall says it's 1:00 a.m. He's still buttoned into his chef coat.

"Are you just coming home from the restaurant?"

"Yeah, I...I didn't think you wanted to see me, so..."

"So you stayed." I sit up so I don't have to glare at him sideways. "I don't get it. I thought tonight was—"

"It was. It still can be." He smiles again, more confident this time. "Come home with me. I can still make dinner. You look...perfect in this dress."

I want to. Go home with him. After all of this, I want to curl up next to him in the front seat of his car and drive to his apartment and be with him. It's hard to stay mad at Warren. But I know it won't be the same as if he'd kept our plans. I know that I'll spend the whole time thinking about how he chose the restaurant over me, and I don't want our first time together to be filled with resentment.

I have so many things I want to say to him, but the only words that come out are, "It was hers."

He frowns and then his face drops when he understands. "Your mom's?"

"Yeah. One of the things she left behind. I was saving it for something special."

"God, Yvonne. I'm sorry." He swallows. Reaches into his pocket and produces a folded piece of paper that he hands me. "I know this doesn't make up for what happened, but I got you something."

I slowly unfold the paper and stare at it, puzzled. It looks like a receipt.

"It's tickets. To the orchestra. The L.A. Phil. I tried to get opening night, but they were already sold out. This is close, though. Just a week later."

I love the L.A. Philharmonic, and I don't go often enough. It's not easy to persuade nonmusicians to go listen to classical music, and going with people in my orchestra has never been any fun. They dissect everything in real time, and it's hard to just sit there and enjoy the music.

"I'm not..."

His eyes search mine for the missing words. "You're not what?"

"Nothing." I haven't told Warren about my talk with Ortiz, and I don't want to. It's embarrassing to admit that you're not good enough at what you thought you wanted to someone who's one of the best in his field. "Thank you." I fold the paper again and set it on my nightstand.

"You don't have to take me," he says. "But I hope you go."

I don't say anything and I don't look at him. His eyes are too sincere. I know he's truly sorry, but I'm not in the mood for apologies right now. I just want to go back to bed and wake up to a new day.

"Happy birthday, Yvonne." He leans in to kiss me and I turn my face so his lips brush my cheek.

He closes the door behind him and I instantly snap off the lamp and slide back under the covers, still wearing my mother's dress.

But before I can drift off, I hear my father's voice in the hallway.

"...still upset?"

"I think she's pretty mad, yeah." Warren sighs.

"Aw, come on. She'll get over it, right? It's been a long day.... Want a smoke?"

I squeeze my eyes shut. If Warren says yes, I will kill him. It's the one thing I've told him I don't want him doing. I don't care if he smokes pot—we both do, and together sometimes—but I don't want him doing that with my dad. Sometimes I wonder if the weed is an excuse for my father's detachment, a cloak that makes it okay for him to disappear while pretending he's still here. I don't want the same thing to happen to Warren.

Warren's pause is much too long, but eventually he says, "Nah, I'm good, Sinclair. See you tomorrow."

I'm still awake when the pungent smoke from my father's pipe floats across the house and into my room.

8.

I sleep late the next day, and then I stay in bed
even longer.

Saturday mornings used to be reserved for Denis. My father
hated it, because he was still sleeping when my instructor arrived
at 10:00 a.m. sharp. But Denis was inflexible with the time. He
had a full roster, he liked to remind me, and if we weren't happy
with the time slot, he was sure he could find someone else who'd
be pleased to take it. My father got earplugs.

I wonder who has my old slot now. I look across the room at
my violin case gathering dust, wedged between the wall and my
backpack. I think of how there was a stretch of years where I practiced every single day. How I never felt quite right if I didn't pick

the violin up at least once each day, even if I only practiced scales. I remember so much about my weekly routine over the years, yet I still can't recall the moment I fell out of love with violin.

I pick up my phone. There's a text from Warren that I ignore. I go to my contacts and scroll through until I find Omar. He didn't put in a last name. Just Omar. I wonder what he and Keely do when they're not performing on the beach. Maybe they don't hang out at all when they're not playing or practicing, but I know better than that. There was a comfort between them that you can't get from simply seeing someone at work or school every day.

I chew my lip, still staring at the screen. I've thought about him a lot since I saw him last week, but this is the first time I've pulled up his number.

Before I can stop myself, I text him.

> Hi.

And then, because I realize I never gave him my number:

> It's Yvonne. From the beach.

I immediately shove the phone under the covers. So dumb. What if he doesn't remember me? He must meet a million girls at the beach every day. Maybe he's even met more than one Yvonne.

My phone buzzes by my thigh and my heart races with it. He must remember me if he's responding so quickly.

But it's a phone call, not a text. And it's Sabina.

"How are you feeling?" she asks when I pick up. Her voice is croaky like it always is the morning after she's been drinking.

"How many drinks did you have last night?"

"Don't ask," she groans.

"What happened after I left?"

"Tequila. Way too much tequila. So...you're okay?"

"I'm all right."

"Want to come over for dinner?" she says. "The mothers want to see you. Then I thought we could go to your house? I'll bring the leftover booze from last night."

"That sounds perfect. I can bring cake."

"Oh God." She groans again. "Dame thought it would be funny to get one of those huge birthday sheet cakes from Costco before he realized you weren't coming. We *destroyed* it. I think I'm still in a sugar coma."

"I kind of destroyed a cake last night, too," I say, thinking of the ganache smeared into the linoleum of Warren's kitchen.

"What?"

"Uh...I'll explain later."

Sabina yawns. "I'm going back to bed. Come over at six thirty."

69

I stop in the bathroom to pee and brush my teeth, then head to the kitchen. I'm surprised to find my father sitting at the table with a cup of coffee and a slice of my cake in front of him.

"You made this?" he asks, pointing his fork at the half-eaten piece.

"Yeah. I felt like baking last night." I grab a cup and fill it with coffee, then lean against the counter, looking at him from across the room. "I needed to clear my head."

He nods, and I think he's not going to say anything else, just go back to reading something on his phone, like usual. Anything to avoid an actual conversation. Especially here, at the house, where he can't hide in a hot, busy kitchen, barking orders instead.

But then he looks at me and says, "I didn't know you had plans last night. I wouldn't have called Warren in."

"But he asked off. Didn't you think about why?"

"I guess I didn't put the two things together, Yvonne." He taps his fork against the plate a couple of times. "I'm not entirely clear on what's going on between you two."

I move to the table. Cautiously, because I'm worried that once I decide to sit down, he'll clam up.

"Neither of you talk to me about the other, so I figured it's none of my business," my father says, shrugging.

Lots of things aren't a parent's business, but from what I hear, that doesn't stop most of them from firmly inserting themselves. I take a sip of coffee. My father and I drink ours the same way: black.

"I don't know what's going on with me and Warren, but after last night...I don't know what I want to happen."

"Well...relationships are hard."

My face flushes. "We're not in a relationship."

"I mean all relationships are hard. I'm better with food."

He's not wrong about that. Even the birthday card he gave me was impersonal; he signed only DAD under the pre-printed birthday message. Staring at the cash that was stuffed inside, I couldn't stop thinking how I would have given that up for him to write LOVE before DAD. I know he loves me, but I'd like to hear it sometimes. The words rolled easily off my mother's tongue, but even when she was here, my father didn't follow her example.

He clears his throat. "You made this cake from scratch?"

"No box needed."

"Frosting, too?"

I purse my lips. "Dad."

"It's very good, Yvonne." As if to prove his point, he crams in a huge mouthful. After he swallows, he says, "I didn't know you could bake like this."

"The recipe is simple." I focus on the place mat under my coffee cup as I say, "It's the one she always used to make my birthday cakes."

"I don't remember it being so good."

I know he means it as a compliment. It's probably one of the best he could ever give, but it makes me sad all the same. She's been gone long enough that he doesn't remember her version. If he can get over her by now, why can't I?

I've been going to Sabina's house for years now, but her moms still fret when they serve me a meal.

"I know this doesn't hold up to what you're used to eating, but I hope you like it," Mama Jess says, passing me the platter of grilled branzino.

"This looks amazing." I put some of the flaky white fish on my plate and pass it on to Sabina. "I don't think my dad's ever made a whole fish. Not at home, anyway."

"I don't like that you leave the head on." Sabina wrinkles her nose. "It's staring at me."

"He doesn't really have a lot of time to cook at home these days," I continue in the light-hearted voice I've learned to adopt over the years whenever I talk about him. I don't have to use it in front of Sabina's parents, but it's instinct.

"Oh, that reminds me—did Sabina tell you Jess and I went to your father's restaurant a couple of weeks ago?" Sabina's other mother, the woman she calls Mom and I call Cora, asks as she spreads a napkin over her lap. They use cloth napkins in Sabina's house. Every day, not just when they have guests.

"How was it?" I slide a large spoonful of roasted vegetables onto my plate.

"Perfect." Mama Jess closes her eyes and lets out a sigh. "That veal is so incredible I don't even feel bad about eating it."

"The service was really great, too," Cora says. "The chef even came over to our table to say hello."

"My dad?"

"No, a young man." Cora takes a sip of wine. "He went around to all the tables. Cute guy."

"Oh, that was probably Warren," I say.

Sabina rolls her eyes.

I still haven't looked at his texts. Which reminds me that I haven't heard back from Omar. My legs itch to walk down the hall and check my phone in Sabina's room, but I force myself to remain still.

"Who's Warren?" Mama Jess looks back and forth between Sabina and me.

"A dummy who doesn't realize how good he has it," Sabina grumbles. She grabs a bit of fish with her fingers and pops it into her mouth.

I pinch her thigh under the table. Sabina glares.

"He's my dad's sous chef," I say. "*SoCal Weekly* is doing an article on him."

"Well, please tell your father—both of them—how much we enjoyed the meal," Cora says.

"The overall experience," adds Mama Jess.

After dinner, they surprise me with a beautiful home-made flan. Sabina sticks a candle into the custardy center and I blow it out, making a wish as I do. It's the day after my birthday and none of my wishes have ever come true, but I figure it can't hurt to try.

Back at my house, Sabina plunks a canvas bag of liquor bottles onto the kitchen counter and declares, "I'm making punch."

"Since when do you know how to make punch?"

"I don't. Someone made it last night, and I'm going to do my best to recreate it."

I watch her get to work, already terrified of her concoction. "Who was there last night?"

"Everybody. Nobody. *Cody* was there."

"Still objectively hot?"

"If you're into the Disney prince sort of look...sure."

Cody was my first, and we had sex three times. I met him at Damon's right around this time last year, when every party was filled to bursting because the summer was over and everyone was together again. Cody does look like a Disney prince, but I found out after he started flirting with me in the kitchen that he was funny, too. I had kissed a couple of guys before him, but I knew by the way my whole body tingled when he brushed his fingers against my arm that I wanted much more with Cody.

Later, he found me waiting in line for the bathroom, and when it was my turn, he went in with me. We made out until people began pounding on the door, then we took our swollen lips to an empty bedroom. Cody was clumsy at almost everything besides kissing, and neither of us really knew what we were doing. But I liked being with him—the hardness of his body pressed against the curves of mine, and the warmth between us. It was the first time I realized someone could make me breathless with a simple touch.

Maybe it was weird to want to talk to a mother about my first time, but I wished I at least had the option. I told Sabina, but it wasn't the same. I wanted someone—*my mother*—to be wary of my actions but proud that I was telling her. I wanted to show her *Look, I'm growing up so fast, you probably don't even recognize me.* But the only person I had was my father, and that was too weird. He'd made it clear from our one and only talk that ever referenced sex that his main concern was I used protection. We'd done that.

Sabina makes a punch that is deceptively smooth, and we fill two ceramic mugs to the brim, then head with them to the backyard.

"Careful," I say as we pass through the sunroom on our way out. I don't know why. If we spill, we could easily clean it up. The carpet is thin and dark. But it feels strange to be in my father's area—even just passing through, I feel as if I'm invading a part of the house that doesn't belong to me.

Outside, Sabina climbs into the hammock first and when I manage to join her without either of us toppling over or spilling our punch, we cheer to the midnight-blue sky.

"A toast to your birthday," Sabina says, gingerly touching the rim of her mug to mine. "How does it feel to be eighteen?"

"Not much different." I take a sip of punch, then rest the mug on my stomach, holding tight with both hands. "Except that now I feel like I should have it all figured out, when I actually feel more confused than I did two years ago."

"I'm kind of jealous," Sabina says. "Not that you're feeling confused, but a little *less* direction would be nice. My applications are completely done, and it's not even October."

Cora wanted her to apply early decision, so she made Sabina start them during the summer. Cora graduated from Dartmouth and has been obsessed with Sabina going to an Ivy League practically since Sabina could hold a pen. Sabina, however, could not be less interested, and her list includes only liberal arts colleges and HBCUs.

"I think it's kind of nice that she's so involved," I say.

Before I talked to him last week, my father and I have had only a couple of vague conversations about college. He's always seemed convinced that I'll figure it out by myself; he's like that with most things about me, actually.

"What if..." I've never said this out loud, and I consider

keeping it to myself. Once I put it out there, neither of us can pretend that I didn't say it, that it's not something I maybe once wanted. "What if I just didn't?"

"Didn't what?"

"Fill out applications."

"What, like take a year off? I mean, it's not what I thought you'd do, but it's something people *do*." Sabina bends her neck awkwardly to take a drink from her mug without sloshing it over the side. "I still can't believe you're not going to play in college."

"Do I seem like the same person?"

"Huh?" Her voice is becoming more relaxed. Lazy, almost.

"I mean . . . who am I without violin?"

"I've never known you without that thing strapped to your back every day," she says. "You couldn't even sleep over on Friday nights because you had to be ready for Denis every week. But you never seemed like one of those people who lives and breathes it, you know?"

I don't know whether to be mad that she noticed or happy that she really does know me so well.

"I used to be. I think."

Sabina turns to face me, and the hammock swings too quickly back and forth. We freeze up like mannequins, squeezing our mugs for dear life.

"The thing is, I wasn't that upset when Denis canceled our lessons," I say when the swaying finally slows. "I mean, I knew it wasn't a good thing to be dropped by your teacher of eleven years. But I was more upset that I wouldn't get to see him every week."

"I thought you hated Denis."

"I did, a little bit." It was more of a love-hate relationship—on both sides, I think. "But it's hard to hate someone who shows up every week, you know? Our routine... it was nice."

No matter how early I had to be up and ready to practice, sacrificing one of my weekend mornings for years, I liked knowing that Denis would be there. Even though my father was paying him ("handsomely," Dad sometimes grumbled as he wrote a check), it was comforting to know that for an hour and a half each week, someone was paying attention to only me. Making time just for me.

We are quiet for a while, the alcohol warming our limbs against the coolness of the evening air. I could fall asleep here, and I wonder if maybe we will, because Sabina isn't moving and her breathing is slowing and then I think maybe it's a bad idea because all the alcohol is still sitting out on the counter—

My phone buzzes, scaring Sabina so badly that she spills punch all over her top.

"Shit!" She tosses the mug to the grass and steps out of the hammock without tipping me over, too. Barely.

"Sorry." I set my own mug on the ground and pull the phone from my pocket.

"Oh my God." Sabina squints at the phone over my shoulder. "I ruined my shirt because of a text from *Warren*?"

"He's been apologizing all day."

"I'm going inside to throw this in the wash," she says, holding her wet shirt away from her body.

As Sabina walks up to the back door, I scroll through the texts I've been getting from Warren since this morning.

> I feel like shit about last night. I'm so sorry. Let me make it up to you?

> I still owe you that dinner. Come over tomorrow night?

> Or come over tonight. I just want to see you.

I read his words over and over, and I'm mad that a part of me wants to see him, too. I'm worried that I'll take him up on his offer, so I back out of Warren's messages and scroll through my most recent ones.

I still haven't heard from Omar. I guess he was just being nice, giving me his number. At least he didn't lead me on, but I can't help feeling stupid for putting myself out there. For thinking maybe he could help me understand my relationship with music... or help me become excited about it again. We don't even know each other.

I open up the message I sent to him this morning.

NOT DELIVERED

How did I not notice this earlier? I sigh, relieved that he isn't ignoring me, and resend. That same red notification pops up immediately.

I think back to the last time I saw him, how he seemed like he really did want to talk to me again. Not like I was a burden, or like I deserved the looks Keely was giving me. He seemed just as intrigued by me as I am by him.

Then I remember something else—what he said: *Call me. Anytime, Yvonne.*

Call.

I don't talk to anyone on the phone besides Warren and Sabina. My dad, sometimes, when it's quicker than texting. It makes me anxious, all the awkward pauses and never knowing when it's the right time to say good-bye.

But then, because Sabina is gone and I'm a bit drunk on vodka punch, I press the little phone icon next to Omar's name.

It rings and rings and—

"Hello?"

I clear my throat. "Omar?"

"Yeah, who's this?" His voice is wary, reminding me of my father's anytime an unfamiliar number shows up on his phone.

"Yvonne. I met you—"

"*Yvonne.* I was hoping I'd hear from you."

I smile, happy to have his warm voice in my ear.

9.

Aside from Sunday breakfast, there is one day of each month that I know I'll see my father, without fail: dinner with Lou.

I'm always included, but I often wonder why he can't set aside that same kind of time for me. Not a breakfast he prepares for himself and shares with me if I make it to the table while it's still hot, but a designated time to hang out and catch up.

I don't remember when the dinners started, but I look forward to them. It's funny seeing my father around Lou. My grandparents died before my mom took off, and I think Dad looks up to Lou like a father.

He still owns the restaurant where he taught Dad everything

he knows, but shortly after my father opened up his own place, Lou handed off the operations to an executive chef. He stops in once a week or so to check on things, but he spends most of his time now playing golf and traveling and cooking in his sprawling house in hilly Mount Washington.

He squeezes me into a big hug at the front door and, like usual, I feel like the little girl I was when I met him. He's my godfather; I guess, in a way, Lou has always felt like a grandpa to me.

Inside, the house smells like garlic and yeast and fresh basil. Lou is wearing the gray T-shirt he always puts on when he cooks instead of an apron. It's splattered with dark streaks of sauces and oils, some fresh and some stained into the material.

He still makes me Shirley Temples. It's kind of sweet and kind of embarrassing because I wonder if he knows I've pretty much tasted the entire spectrum of alcohol at this point. Still, he makes his own grenadine, and the Shirley Temples are just as delicious now as they were in sixth grade.

Lou pours himself and my father glasses of dark red wine and we take the drinks out to his second-floor deck while his Bolognese sauce simmers on the stove.

"Man, you are living the life," Dad says, staring out at the incredible view from the hill. Lou's backyard overlooks the skyline of downtown Los Angeles in the distance, and the sunsets here are so beautiful they don't appear real. Pink and lavender skies with puffy clouds dotting the horizon.

"It's not a bad one." Lou clinks our glasses in cheers before he sips his wine. "You ready for this semiretirement life?"

"Never," Dad says, and I don't think he's joking.

Lou raises a bushy white eyebrow. "Sinclair, you know that industry will work you like a dog if you let it."

My father shrugs. "And you know I like the pressure."

"Well, never say never," Lou says. "This is a *very* good life." He turns to me. "And how are things with my Yvonne?"

"I'm fi—" I start to say, but before I can finish, Lou jumps up, snapping his fingers.

"Hold that thought. I'll be right back."

I look at my dad, who shrugs. A breeze floats over, sending the sweet scent of the Meyer lemon tree below wafting up to the balcony.

Lou returns with a small, wrapped box and a thick envelope. "Happy birthday, sweetheart," he says, leaning down to kiss my cheek.

I wish they weren't both looking at me, because I feel like I might cry. Lou doesn't owe me anything, but even he cares about me more than my mother does.

"Open it," he urges, easing back into the seat between my father and me.

I open the card first, an oversize one with swirly letters, flowers, and sugary-sweet words that he signed with LOVE, LOU at the bottom. I look a bit too long at the word *love*. The wrapping paper peels easily off the package, revealing a small velvet box. I snap it open to find a delicate gold pin in the shape of a Stradivarius violin. The detailing is exquisite, down to the tiny replica of the fingerboard. I slip it out of the box and onto my palm, running my index finger over the tiny lines and curves.

"It's vintage," Lou says when I still haven't spoken. "And it looks really well made, but if you don't like—"

And then I do start to cry. Not an onslaught of tears— just a single one that drips onto my wrist. I quickly brush it away, hoping Lou won't notice. But Lou notices everything.

"You don't have to keep it if you don't like it, Yvonne," he says in that borderline frantic voice people use when tears appear. "I just thought it was something you might like."

"I love it. I do. I just...this isn't my future anymore."

Lou frowns. "Oh, Yvonne. I'm sorry to hear that. I can take it back."

I pause for a moment to wonder why he accepted the idea so easily. Clearly he still associates me with violin, but what if he knew I wasn't good enough to go anywhere with it? He's heard me play plenty of times, sometimes on request. But what if my growing disinterest and lack of improvement was apparent to everyone, and they've been humoring me this whole time?

"No." I shake my head. "It's beautiful."

Lou squeezes my shoulder. "If you change your mind, I won't be offended."

My father has stayed quiet during this exchange, but now he looks over. "You know, Yvonne is shaping up to be quite the baker."

"It was one cake." I down the rest of my Shirley Temple in one gulp.

"One very good cake."

"Oh, really?" Lou gives me a small smile. "Looking to go into your pops's line of business?"

"What? No!"

On the other side of him, Dad laughs.

"I mean, I'm just not interested in cooking...or restaurants."

"Baking isn't cooking, though," Lou says thoughtfully. "Pastry chefs have a different skill set than other restaurant chefs."

"Pastry chef? I think that's a little premature." I glance at my father to see if he's mentioned this to Lou before this evening, but he doesn't look like he's hiding anything.

"Well, there's only one way to find out." The slight smile from earlier now stretches all the way across Lou's face. "I want you to bake me a cake."

"You're putting me to work?"

"Just asking for a favor. I'll choose the cake and give you the recipe. You make it and bring it over."

That's not such a bad deal. The pastry chef talk is too much, but I do like baking. I can't forget how it calmed me when I was so upset the other night. And I can't ignore how nice it feels to hear my father's praise. But it was one time. One cake. And the whole experience was steeped in nostalgia, down to the recipe recorded in my mother's handwriting on a card she must have touched dozens of times.

But it will give me something to think about besides the fact that every time I have to explain how I'm losing my connection to violin, I feel like I'm losing a part of me.

"Okay," I say. "Deal."

My gaze falls on my father. He smiles before he takes another sip of wine. It's small, but I see it.

After dinner, Dad goes to fiddle with Lou's espresso maker while Lou and I clear the dishes.

"Any boyfriends I should know about?" Lou asks, stacking my plate on top of his. He asks every so often, but it still surprises me that he invites that type of talk between us. No matter what my father suspected was going on with Warren and me all this time, he was wholly uncomfortable discussing us in the context of a couple.

"Nobody special," I say automatically.

I wonder if my answer would have been Warren if things had gone differently on my birthday.

There is Omar. Thinking of him makes me smile. Because as much as I care about Warren, he confuses me. I know his feelings for me are real, but actions should speak the loudest, and I'm still disappointed by how my birthday turned out. He has more responsibilities than ever since his promotion, but I don't want to start off a relationship believing he cares more about his job than me. I've had enough of that in my life. I wasn't important enough for my mother to stick around, and my father has chosen work first for as long as I can remember.

Omar and I didn't talk long last night. He sounded like he was in the middle of something. There were voices in the background—a lot of them. I kept listening to see if I could hear the sound of the ocean waves behind him or maybe Keely tuning her viola. I couldn't tell where he was and I was too shy to ask, but he seemed pleased to hear from me. I actually flushed with happiness when he suggested we hang out this week.

"Not that there's any rush," Lou adds quickly, breaking into my thoughts. "I didn't meet Claud until I was thirty-five."

He smiles at me as he takes the dishes into the kitchen.

I never know how to feel when Lou brings up Claudia. She was the love of his life, and she died from cervical cancer three years ago. I always feel a bit ashamed for thinking this, but sometimes I believe it would be easier to accept my mother leaving if she'd been sick.

If she hadn't made the choice to leave on her own.

10.

Omar asked me to meet him down at the beach, and I don't think I've been to Venice as much in the last three years as I have in the last three weeks. But when I think of his eyes, his dreads, the way he said my name on the phone—I don't mind.

As I drive, I wonder what we'll do tonight. He kept plans vague, only confirming the time and where to meet on the beach. Maybe we'll walk over to Abbot Kinney and look at all the overpriced boutiques before we grab a bite to eat. Or maybe we can go over to the Venice Canals—I've never been, but it's supposed to be amazing, with breathtaking houses and lush gardens along the water.

My heart thumps faster as I near his usual spot on the

boardwalk. I expect to see him finishing up a set, but their chairs are gone and Keely is nowhere to be found. It's just Omar, standing alone, with his back to the boardwalk as he looks out toward the ocean.

His dreads are pulled into a low and messy bun, and I don't think it's likely, but they seem even more sun-kissed than the last time I saw him. The golden strands wink under the late-afternoon light fading over the water. I want to touch each one of them. I've never known anyone with such beautiful locs.

He turns around before I reach him, as if he knew I was coming. His smile is easy and it makes my knees shaky, but I remember the deep breathing Mama Jess taught Sabina and me when we did yoga in their living room. How she said I could use it to calm myself throughout the day. And it works. By the time I reach him, I feel more like myself and less like a Yvonne-shaped tangle of nerves.

He gives me a quick hug and it takes me so much by surprise that I almost forget Omar is *touching* me and I need to take in every detail to report back to Sabina. Like how he smells of sandalwood and how his hair is soft against my skin as a couple of errant locs brush my neck.

"Thanks for coming down," he says, still smiling. "Hope it wasn't too much trouble. You live near downtown, right?"

"Yeah, Highland Park. And it's no big deal." I shrug. "I like driving, and my dad pays for my gas."

I don't know why I said that last part, and Omar laughs at the face I can't stop myself from making.

"It's okay. You still live at home—you should let your parents pay for whatever they will for as long as they can. Parents are supposed to take care of their kids."

I grin. "I'll remind him of that the next time I ask for money. So, what are we doing?"

"Are you hungry? Best burgers in Venice are just down that way on the boardwalk." He pauses, then squints at me. "You're not a vegetarian, are you?"

I shake my head. "I'm vegan."

His eyebrows shoot so high I burst out laughing.

"Kidding. My dad's a chef. That's not really allowed at my house."

He nudges me good-naturedly in my side and I can't stop smiling and then we're heading down to the part of the board-walk where I rarely go, palm trees lined up along one side like fifty-foot statues.

The burger place is small, crowded, and hot. It smells like grease and fried cheese and my mouth waters as soon as we step through the doorway. The space in front of the register is so tight that Omar and I have to stand with our shoulders touching. I try to pretend that I don't notice as I gaze at the chalk-board menu behind the counter.

"There are only four choices?"

"See, those fancy burger spots are a scam," Omar says, shaking his head. "This is all you need. Meat, bread, cheese."

My father has always said simple food is better, and Lou preaches the same philosophy. So maybe Omar is right, but I must appear skeptical because he laughs.

"I promise you won't be disappointed."

We both order cheeseburgers and split an order of crinkle fries. I offer to pay, but Omar waves at me like "forget it," pulling a beat-up leather wallet from his back pocket. The girl who takes his money says someone will bring out our burgers as she gives us our drinks.

We find an empty table, squeezed into a corner. And what seems like barely a minute later, a guy with shaggy blond hair shuffles over in Birkenstocks, carrying our order.

"My man O!" He sets the food on the table. "Didn't know you were stopping in tonight."

Omar stands to greet him and they give each other one of those half-hug, half-handshake things. "Yvonne's never been here—had to show her the best grill on the beach. Yvonne, this is Calvin. He owns the place."

Calvin gives me a friendly hello, then looks at Omar again. "No Keely today?"

Omar's voice is friendly when he responds, but something changes in his eyes. A tenseness that wasn't there before. "No Keely."

"Ah...right." Calvin's neck turns red: the confirmation I needed that Keely and Omar once had something going on. "All right, man, you better get to that burger before it gets cold. Don't want you making any complaints to the kitchen." He turns to me. "Nice meeting you. Stop in anytime—any friend of Omar's, you know?"

"Nice meeting you, too."

We eat silently for a couple of minutes, and Omar is right. The burger is simple but also one of the best I've had in a long time. It's juicy with gooey, melted cheese and a perfectly toasted bun. Every bite is a little piece of heaven.

"Ketchup?" I hold the red squeeze bottle over the basket of fries.

He nods. "I'm glad you're here. That you called. I don't always remember to tell people that my phone doesn't get texts."

"Probably half the people I know wouldn't talk to anyone if they couldn't text." I don't admit that vodka punch was the only reason I got up the courage to call.

"Keely hates how basic my phone is," he says. "But I don't need it for anything except calling people."

Keely again.

"So." He leans back with one arm draped over his chair. "You gonna tell me about this music thing?"

"How much do you want to hear?" I am suddenly shy.

Even though this is the reason we're supposedly here in the first place.

"It's usually best to start at the beginning," he says with a smile.

I tell him how I was good enough for Denis to take me on as a student when I was seven years old. Good enough to represent our school at local competitions. Good enough to think I could play professionally—even if I knew I'd never be the best in the symphony—until I was forced to confront the reality that I don't have enough talent *or* passion.

"So now everything's fucked," he says when I stop talking.

I finish chewing and set down the little bit left of my burger. "Yeah. I have no idea what to do. I think about quitting the orchestra so I can give it up altogether, but then I don't know if I can. I've been playing for eleven years. How can I just give up something that used to mean so much to me?"

"I know exactly how you feel." Omar wipes his mouth with a napkin and crumples the wrapper from his burger, tossing it into the empty fry basket. "And I think we'd better discuss it somewhere else, because those people across the room are staring us down for this table."

Back on the beach, we cross the lumpy sand to walk close to the water. The air is cool and the moisture in the breeze settles over my arms and face like a second skin, but I don't pull out the sweater I brought.

"So, you know I went to Berklee," Omar says, picking up where we left off.

"Did you love it?"

"I hated it. Dropped out after my first year."

"Did you go somewhere else?"

"No. I realized school—and classical music—weren't for me. It wasn't Berklee. I really liked it there."

"But how were you able to quit? You were on your way to being a professional. The people who trained me don't even think I'm good enough to audition for music programs."

He sticks his hands in his pockets as we wander slowly down the beach. "It wasn't easy. But I knew that I was doing what I loved every day next to some of the best musicians I'd ever heard and I was deeply unhappy."

"So you just *quit*?" I've been thinking about walking into Ortiz's office and doing the same thing, but I can never go through with it. Maybe because I've never quit anything, but I think it's deeper than that. I know what it's like to be left behind, and even though my violin is an inanimate object, I feel guilty when I think about giving it up forever—abandoning the one thing that's always been there for me.

"Yeah, I traveled around, checking out some places I'd never been. And I kept noticing all the street musicians.... How no matter where I went, a lot of them were just as good as the people I'd been in school with. Some of them were better. There are people out there playing everything you can think of—cellos, saxophones, accordions and shit."

"You knew that's what you wanted to do right away?"

"Nah. Even if they were better, I was still trained to think I was too good for that, you know?"

Before I heard him playing with Keely, I felt the same way about street performers. I wondered why they didn't just take their talent somewhere legitimate instead of busking for loose change.

"But I started talking to some of them, and then, before I knew it, I was bringing my fiddle with me. Eventually I started to play with some of them and..." He spreads his arms out in the direction of the boardwalk as if to say "here I am." "I teach, too."

"Where?"

"At the Cooper Youth Center, on Tuesdays and Thursdays. The pay barely puts a dent in my rent money, but it's worth it."

"Cooper Youth Center? The one downtown?"

His eyebrows go up. "You know it?"

"Yeah, my dad did a program with them last year through his work." The kids are mostly from low-income families, and he had some of his employees teach a few cooking classes at the center. He even showed up himself one day, and a community paper did a small piece on the partnership.

He brushed it off like it was no big deal, but I saw the pride in his eyes when he read the paper.

"I like it there. The kids are great. But this is my favorite place to be."

"How did you meet Keely?" I don't look over because I don't want to see his eyes change the way they did when he was talking to Calvin.

Neither of us said this was a date, but walking along the quickly emptying beach next to him sure makes it feel like one. And maybe he's just a generous guy, but he paid for my meal, too.

"She was here first," he replies. "But I actually saw her at a show she did at the Hotel Café."

"That's kind of huge."

"Yeah, it wasn't her show, but she played strings for another act. I stuck around to talk to her and we vibed really well so we played together to see if we were any good. She was already set up here on the boardwalk. She asked if I wanted to join her, and we've been together ever since."

"You sound so good together," I say, even though I don't want to acknowledge that anything about them together is good.

"Thanks. Listen, Yvonne, I don't want to be weird or anything, but I thought you should know..." He pauses. "Keely and I used to date. And we're still roommates, and obviously we still work together. But we're not *together* together. We still have a good vibe, musically, and people know us as a team. So it didn't make sense to split up. But I don't want to be with her. Just so you know."

"Oh." I hesitate, trying to think of something mature or profound or breezy to say, but all I can think of is, "Okay."

He stops and touches my arm so I'll look at him. "I don't want to make you uncomfortable, but I'm kind of an up-front guy."

"I'm not uncomfortable." A sharp, cold gust of air blows through. I shiver. "I wanted to know, I just didn't want to ask. Or assume something was here that isn't. . . ."

When he sees I'm still shivering, he reaches out and rubs my arms with his hands. They're callused, but dry and warm. Soon I'm shivering from his touch alone. It's been a long time since anyone but Warren has touched me in a way that made me feel like this—that makes me want more.

"I didn't want to assume anything, either," he says, his hands moving slower and slower. They stop at my elbows. "But I know that I like talking to you. And I'd like to get to know you better."

I can't hold back the smile that breaks out, and I can't keep it from growing as I respond that yes, I would very much like that, too.

"I'm glad," Omar says in a low voice that makes me shiver again—this time down to my toes. He reaches out to push a few braids behind my ears. When he leans forward, I think he's going to kiss me, which seems too soon...except it's not when you feel what I am feeling. Something electric. Even if the person was a complete stranger weeks ago.

His mouth stops by my ear. "If you want to quit violin, make sure you're quitting for you. Don't ever let anyone tell you there's a right or wrong way to feel about your music."

I exhale into the cool, salty air.

11.

I've never gone this long without talking to Warren.

I thought maybe he'd forgo Sunday breakfast because of the tension, but the doorbell rings right on time, just as I'm savoring my first cup of coffee. Dad asks me to get the door, claiming he's too busy prepping his frittata.

I twist my braids up into a topknot and take a quick look in the entryway mirror before I open the front door.

Warren looks good, and I hate that.

We stand there looking at each other for a long moment until he finally says, "Can I come in?"

I close the door behind him.

"How's it going?" He's standing awkwardly when I turn

to look at him, as if he hasn't been in this house or in my presence hundreds of times before.

"Fine." I pause, but I don't have anything else to say to him right now. "Dad's in the kitchen."

Warren nods and heads down the hall without another word. After a couple of seconds, I follow.

He immediately rolls up his sleeves and washes his hands so he can help Dad. I think it's instinct now—like he can't *not* get involved when he's in the kitchen. Dad doesn't mind, but only because it's Warren. He spends way more time at work than here, but he won't let anyone near his kitchen. I think I get the privilege only because I live here.

"Hey, Sinclair, got any tips for this interview I have coming up?" Warren's back is to my father as he shaves ribbons of asparagus off the stalk. "I'm talking to that reporter from *SoCal Weekly* in a few days."

"Don't say anything you don't want to get out," Dad says right away. He's chopping scallions into superthin slices on a thick wooden cutting board. I don't think I'll ever get tired of watching his knife work. He's not particularly flashy, but he's fast and consistent and he always makes the precision look so easy.

"Oh, yeah? You speak from experience?"

Dad glances over at me before he responds, but I don't look up from my phone.

"They started asking a bunch of personal questions," he

says gruffly. "I got defensive and that gave them more to write about than if I had told them to move on to something else."

They must have been asking about my mother. Dad is private, but he wouldn't have been defensive if they had asked about me—he's talked about me in the few interviews he's granted.

"Noted. Is it normal to be this nervous? I—shit!" Warren drops the vegetable peeler and holds one of his knuckles up to his face.

Dad turns around. "Bad one?"

"Nah, but I should put something on it."

I stand before my father can look at me again. "We have a first-aid kit in the bathroom. Come on."

Warren holds his finger under the faucet in the bathroom sink, sending pink water swirling down the drain. Next to him, I open the kit and pull out antiseptic wipes, bandages, and gauze.

"How bad is it?"

"I don't think I'll need gauze." He holds up his knuckle so I can see the nick.

I unwrap the wipes and bandage and watch him clumsily clean and cover up the wound.

"Looks like I'll live," he says as I put away the kit.

"Lucky you." I toss the wrappers into the trash and am about to leave the bathroom when he touches my shoulder.

"Yvonne."

I turn around to face him, unsmiling. "What?"

"I miss you."

"Warren—"

"I do. I'm really, really sorry about what happened."

"You don't need to keep apologizing. I hear you."

He lets out a breath. "Then what can I do to make it up to you?"

"I don't want you to do anything. I just want to forget about that night, okay?"

"Does that mean you'll let me make you dinner sometime soon?"

I raise an eyebrow. "I didn't say all that."

Warren laughs. "Fine. Then will you start answering my texts?"

"Maybe."

But when he leans in to hug me, I let him, and I know that regardless of how hard I try, I can't stay mad at Warren. Which is comforting, knowing someone that well. But it's also terrifying. How badly would he have to disappoint me to irreparably damage whatever is going on between us? If I forgive him so easily, will he keep finding new ways to hurt me?

After we devour our first servings and graze over second helpings and drink all the coffee in the pot, we peel ourselves out of our seats. Dad goes off to the sunroom for his postmeal smoke, leaving me alone again with Warren.

"What are you doing today?" he asks.

"Making a cake."

"I thought you hated cake." He gives me a wry smile.

"It's for Lou," I say, ignoring his dig, because we haven't discussed the cake I smashed into his kitchen floor, and I'm not feeling up to it right now.

He frowns. "Sinclair's Lou?"

"He's my Lou, too."

"Why are you making him a cake?"

"Because he and my dad are trying to get my mind off the whole violin thing."

"Oh. You're nervous about auditions?"

That's right—Warren doesn't know. I was too embarrassed after talking to Ortiz, and then the whole birthday thing happened. And it seems so ridiculous. I just told a guy who's hardly more than a stranger exactly how I was feeling. Warren should know, too. He always knows everything that's going on with me. But it's different this time.

"There aren't going to be any auditions. And no offense, Warren, but I don't really want to talk about this." I get up to take my plate and mug to the sink.

He follows me. "You're not going to audition at all?"

I drop my dishes in so carelessly, I'm surprised the porcelain doesn't crack. "I said I don't want to talk about it."

The more I talk about it, the more I feel like a failure.

Did I grow so attached to the *idea* of playing violin that I truly didn't understand my love had faded? Or was I dishonest with myself, shoving the truth down deep when I realized it probably wasn't the path for me?

Warren is behind me and then his hands are on my waist, his cheek against mine. "It's me, Yvonne. You can talk to me about anything."

I whip around, pushing on his chest. Pushing him away from me. "I'm serious, Warren. I especially don't want to talk about it with *you*."

"So things aren't okay with us," he says quietly.

"It's not that." I shake my head. "It's—you're really great at what you do. You always have been. You didn't even go to culinary school!"

"You make it sound like I came out of the womb winning James Beard Awards. I still have so much to learn."

"But you're *great*. Not just good sometimes, or generally okay. That's the difference between you and me." My breath catches at the back of my throat. "So I'm sorry, but I can't talk to you about this, Warren."

The hurt that flashes in his eyes cuts me. It's just a couple of seconds and then they're back to normal, but I don't miss it. I think of how easily I was able to talk to Omar about all of this. And of course it's different, because he knows what it feels like to hold a violin, to spend so much time with the instrument that it's like an extension of you. But I don't know him, no matter how comfortable I feel with him. And it seems like I've known Warren forever.

"Okay." He walks back to the table to collect the rest of the plates. "If you change your mind or need someone...I'm here."

After a few seconds of trying to make myself say something to him and failing each time, I turn around to rinse the breakfast dishes instead.

12.

I have a ritual.

Each year that my birthday comes and goes with no word from my mother, I say that I'll stop. I promise myself that I won't rely on this like a temporary salve for a wound that won't heal.

But just like last year and the year before and the ones before that, I pull out everything I own that reminds me of her.

And then, when I'm done with that, I go to my father's bedroom and retrieve the small box of her things that he keeps hidden at the back of his closet.

This year, I don't feel like being alone when I do it, so I ask Sabina to come over. She doesn't know about it, not really. She knows that I kept a few things that remind me of my mother—like the blue dress I wore on my birthday, and the recipe cards stacked together in the kitchen.

Sabina frowns when she steps into my bedroom and sees everything spread out. "Are you having a garage sale?"

"Have you ever known us to have a garage sale? My father would rather cut off his tongue than haggle with people over shit he doesn't want. This is my mom's stuff, Sabs."

"Oh." Her voice is soft as she slowly approaches the bed, looking but not touching. "Do you remember all of it?"

I do. There's the blue dress, of course, which I remember she once wore to a party because I was there. She and Dad brought me with them, and when it got late I was tucked into a guest room with a huge bed and a TV. I woke up to my mother scooping me into her arms, the lace scratchy against my cheek.

I show Sabina the gold bangles that used to tinkle from my mother's wrists as she'd help me in and out of my car seat, or pour me a glass of water, or make pancakes on the weekends.

Sabina flips carefully through the yellowed pages of my mother's favorite cookbook, the one filled with dessert recipes only. "I didn't know she was a baker."

"I didn't think of her as a baker. I mean, she did bake." A lot, actually. "But I always felt like my dad did the cooking, so that's why she baked. Not because she loved it."

"This has notes in the margins," Sabina observes, stopping

on a recipe for gingerbread cake. "And she clearly used this book a lot. She was a baker, Yvonne."

I think of a few days earlier, when I took a homemade carrot cake to Lou. He sliced into it immediately and ate two pieces right in front of me, praising the texture of the cake and the chopping of the walnuts and the consistency of the cream cheese frosting. Lou is softer around the edges than my father, but he isn't one to bullshit. He was so effusive and kind that I was almost embarrassed, listening to him talk about my skill.

My mother's CD collection is expansive, and she left the whole thing here. Sabina crouches over the box and rifles through, marveling at the stacks of clear plastic cases stuffed with liner notes. "She really liked hip-hop."

"She loved it. All her ticket stubs are from hip-hop shows."

Sabina slides a Brand Nubian CD back into the box. "Do you still think about looking for her?"

"Sometimes. Not like I used to."

Something has always stopped me. I'm not sure what. Maybe knowing how it would upset my father if he ever found out. He doesn't offer up a lot of emotions, and I don't want the one he does show me to be anger. Also... there's a part of me that thinks maybe I won't like what I find.

And now, especially since this big birthday went by with no word from her, I'm starting to wonder why I should bother. She's the one who left, not me. Besides, we haven't moved out of the house she lived in, and even if we had, my father would be easy enough to find.

"Do you still miss her?"

I sit on the floor next to Sabina, cross-legged. "I don't know. I guess I miss having someone around here besides my dad. But I don't... I don't feel like my memories of her are real."

"What? Even with all this stuff she left?"

"That's the thing. It made me feel better at first... the memories. But now they feel manufactured. Like, I look at the bag she left, and I know she carried it every day, but I don't feel anything when I see it or touch it."

Sabina is quiet and when I look over, her eyes are sad. "You know that Mom and Mama Jess love you."

I nod, looking down at my lap.

"And I know you and your dad do okay. But if you ever need anything—"

"I know. Sorry I've been so needy lately. I guess it's just a tough time of year."

"It's not like this is some trivial shit, Yvonne. It's your mom. I get it."

We leave my mother's things spread around my room and go out for ramen in Little Tokyo. The restaurant is busy and loud, with the staff's voices intermingling as they shout out orders and hellos and good-byes.

Sabina surveys the restaurant, sipping from her glass of

water before she looks at me. "Do you think it's weird that I'm a virgin?"

I almost spit out my own water.

She sighs. "I guess that answers my question."

"No, Sabs. I wasn't expecting that. It's not weird," I say firmly, looking into her eyes. "Why?"

"The other night, at Damon's, everyone was telling stories.... So many of them have already slept with more than one person. You texted then, and I was glad to get away because I didn't want to say I haven't had sex yet."

"Well, you're not the only person who isn't having sex," I say. There's a whole group of girls at Courtland who flaunt their purity rings as if virginity is the hot new thing. They mostly stick to themselves, but nobody shuns them.

"I'm not like those girls," she says. "It's not religious for me. And it seems like some of them do it for the attention. Like, they want to be known for not having sex... like that defines you."

Our server slides huge bowls in front of each of us: spicy miso for me, and pork belly ramen for Sabina. I look at her through the curls of steam rising from our dishes, waiting for her to continue.

"I guess I just want to wait for marriage." Sabina swirls her chopsticks through her bowl. "That seems so antiquated, right?"

"No," I say quickly. I never considered that for myself, but I don't think there's anything wrong with it. "All that matters is what you want. And anybody who cares if you're having sex is stupid. It's pretty overrated."

"But you haven't slept with anyone you care about, right? Doesn't that make a difference?"

"Maybe." I guess that would have changed if I'd been with Warren. "It was fine with Cody and Henry....Better with Cody, but I didn't see fireworks."

I met Henry at a Courtland party. He's the cousin of a girl who was in my English class. We didn't so much as kiss that night, but we talked for almost the entire evening and I liked him. With Cody, there was an almost animal attraction, like we couldn't keep our hands off of each other. Henry was more experienced than Cody, but there was no chemistry between us. I didn't feel much of anything when he touched me; it was all sort of mechanical, and I wondered how that was possible when we were so compatible in other ways. We went on a couple of dinner-and-movie dates and slept together twice, and that was that.

"You don't wish you'd waited for Warren?"

I shake my head. "I've thought about it, but that would have felt like too much pressure. Like, what if it wasn't good because it was my first time?"

"I can't believe you've already been with two guys," she says before slurping up a spoonful of broth. Her voice is thoughtful and free of malice, but the words still stab me.

I frown. "What does that mean?"

She looks at me, surprised. "Oh. I didn't mean that in a bad way. I just...I can't imagine letting people touch me who I don't even talk to anymore. And disease and pregnancy... there's so much to think about."

"Sabs, I use protection when I have sex....I'm safe. And people break up. Or get divorced. Marriage doesn't mean you're going to end up with the same person forever."

She may have good role models in her parents, but I know firsthand that promises and legal papers mean nothing if someone decides she doesn't want to be there anymore.

"I know." She pauses. "Sorry. I'm not judging you. We're just different that way."

"I guess we are."

I don't want to be annoyed with her, but it's hard not to think she's judging me after that comment. If she's weirded out by the fact that I've slept with two guys, what will she think when that number increases? I've never thought of sex as shameful. Our school and friends are pretty progressive, and even my father clearly understands that abstinence is a choice, not a way of life for everyone.

"The pork belly is delicious," she says, trying to smooth things over. "Want a bite?"

She pushes her bowl toward me, and I tear off a bit of the meat with my chopsticks.

"So good, right?"

I nod as I chew, and I force myself to give Sabina a smile. Her words came out wrong, that's all.

But it doesn't stop me from feeling like shit.

The house smells like weed. And my father shouldn't be home this early, not unless something is wrong.

I hurry down the hallway to the sunroom, but it's empty. I stop at his room next, but it's dark. My stomach starts to sink when I see the light on in my bedroom.

He's sitting on the floor—knees up, his back against my bed. There's an ashtray next to him with a burned-out joint inside. My mother's things surround him.

"You found the box," he says. He taps his fingers against the one I lugged out from his closet. Sabina and I didn't even get to it before we left.

"I found it a long time ago." I don't know whether to stand or sit. Finally, I drop down into my desk chair.

"I forgot about it." His voice is tinged with disbelief. Almost like he's saying he forgot about her.

I know what's in the box without looking: the flip-flops she used to wear when she went out to get the mail or water the plants on the porch; a half-used jar of the cold cream she slathered on to remove her makeup each night; one lone, dangly earring, a gold-plated feather that's lighter than it looks. There's more, but none of it makes sense together. All of it could be thrown out.

"Why were you looking at this?" He doesn't sound angry, just tired and curious.

"I look at it every year...to remember her, I guess. That she existed. That I'm not making her up."

"Oh, Yvonne."

"I meant to put it back before you got home, but you're never home this early...."

"Slow night. I left Warren in charge." My father sighs. "This isn't the life I wanted for you—to have to look at a box of junk to remember your mother."

"It's not your fault."

He's quiet for a long time and then finally he gets up, clutching the ashtray with one of his big hands. He stands in front of me for a moment, looking out into the hallway at nothing. Then he pats my shoulder with his free hand. I wait for him to say something before he leaves, but he never does.

I look at everything spread around my room like some kind of pathetic vigil. It *is* just junk. Boxes of it.

I spy the cookbook Sabina was flipping through earlier.

Lou sent me home with another assignment: lemon meringue pie this time.

A challenge.

I clear a space on my bed, pick up the book, and flip to the table of contents.

13.

I'm standing outside the address Omar gave me, sure that I have the wrong place.

The street is near the beach, but it appears closer to what Mr. Gamble told us Venice used to look like than anything I've ever seen. The houses aren't scary. Just neglected. Craftsman homes and bungalows with sagging porches and missing shutters that make me sad.

The yard of the house I'm staring at is in need of a good mowing. Weedy vines grow along the porch railing, curling up to the eaves. Light filters through the thin curtains on the front window, and I can see bodies moving inside, but I can't make out if any of them are Omar.

He said to call him when I get here, but now I'm wondering if I should leave. I don't get a *bad* feeling. Just different. It's not like I live behind the gates in Bel Air, but even the oldest parts of my neighborhood look better than this.

Omar makes the choice for me—he walks out the front door as I'm still debating. "Hey!" he calls, beckoning me toward the porch. "Why are you standing out there? Come on in!"

"Sorry." I step off the sidewalk and pick my way through the overgrown lawn, glad it's still too light out for raccoons and skunks to be scuffling around in the long blades of grass. "I didn't know if I had the right house."

"Yeah, it's not much to look at, but it's home for now."

"Oh, I didn't—I mean—"

Omar grins. "Yvonne, it looks like a shithole. You don't have to pretend it doesn't."

He greets me with a quick hug and a kiss on the cheek that I feel long after he pulls away. His lips are soft and warm, and my skin burns when I think about how I'd like to feel them against my own. The earthy scent of sandalwood clings to him; I want to bury my nose in his neck. I had a quick attraction to Cody when we met, but it wasn't the same as this. Being intimate so soon with Cody was primarily fueled by all the alcohol. I've been sober each time Omar and I have talked, but being around him makes me feel a bit drunk, like I'm never sure how I'm going to react.

He opens the door and ushers me in, and I feel like I've been transported to a different world. It's not that there are so many people—but they're all so interesting that my eyes are flitting about wildly, trying to take them all in. It looks like somebody wrapped up Venice Beach itself and shook it out into this house. There are beer-swigging skaters and pierced guys in muscle shirts and skinny, tattooed girls with multi-colored heads and matted strands of hair masquerading as dreadlocks. Several people are holding paper plates of food while squeezing cans of cheap beer under their arms. Everyone looks happy—pleased to be around one another.

Omar leads me through the front room and down the hallway, where we have to thread through the people packing either side.

"Do you guys have a lot of parties?" I ask, raising my voice to be heard above the din.

Omar smiles over his shoulder. "It's not really a party."

We reach the kitchen and he stops in front of a card table packed with food. None of it looks particularly appetizing, but there's a lot of it.

"Want something to eat? Looks like they already killed the mac and cheese."

"No, thanks. I ate before I came." And I feel like a snob, but I probably wouldn't touch any of that food even if I were near starving. "How is this not a party?"

"Well, it's grown. This is probably the most people we've ever had. But it's more of a jam session."

"A *jam* session? That's something people actually do?"

He grins. "Don't look at me like that. Every couple of months, a few of us get together to play. Got a lot of musicians in this group. And a lot of friends who like to come hang."

"Do you, like, rehearse?"

Omar laughs. "That's not how a jam session works. It's all improvised. You know, I should have told you to bring your violin."

"No, I'm—I don't think I'd be very good."

How can I trust my own instincts now? I'm afraid of how badly I'd embarrass myself if I had to play with anyone but my fellow orchestra members. I picture myself freezing up, all of Denis's criticisms and Ortiz's hard truths swirling through my mind instead of the familiar notes I've been playing for years.

"I doubt that." Omar bends down to open a cooler under the table. "Want a beer?"

We both take a can and then he walks me around the downstairs of the house, introducing me to people and showing me all the rooms. After the fifth roommate I meet, I ask how many he has.

"Right now? There's probably about twenty of us here,

give or take a couple. Some people are here only on the weekends." My eyes widen so much that he laughs again. "I take it you've never known anyone who lives in a communal house."

"No...I guess I haven't." I peek into the dining room where a group sits around a long, farmhouse-style table with mismatched benches on either side. A built-in hutch on one wall holds an assortment of dishes stacked and piled into every space possible. There's art on the walls, and though it's a little Gothic for my taste, it gives the room a homey feel. Everything about it looks like a normal dining room until I spy the wall opposite the hutch. "What's that?"

"We have three refrigerators, so we keep the other two in here. They fill up pretty quick—"

"No, on the wall between them."

His attention shifts to the enormous whiteboard that displays a sloppily markered grid.

"Oh, the chore chart. We update it every week. Some people aren't so good about cleaning up."

I keep my mouth shut because I've never had to do chores. Dad expects me to pick up after myself, but he hired someone to professionally clean our house years ago, so it's not like I have to snap on yellow gloves and scrub down the bathroom.

By the time we loop back around to the front of the

house, the chatter has increased to a dull roar. I don't understand how they're ever going to get this many people to quiet
down enough to hear the music. Then, from the middle of
the room, someone lets out a long, shrill whistle, the type
that comes from sticking fingers in your mouth and a whole
lot of practice. The noise eventually trickles down to a few
low murmurs.

"Hey, y'all! We're just about ready to start. All musicians
to the front!"

Before I know what's happening, Omar's fingers are
lightly wrapped around my wrist and he's pulling me forward with him.

"What are you…" But my words are lost as we cut
through the crowd.

And when we get to the front of it, I'm standing
face-to-face with Keely. Her big smile shows off her high
cheekbones, and she looks happier than I've ever seen her at
the boardwalk. I realize with a start that she was the one who
let out that whistle. She's the one taking charge and bringing
everyone together. It's a surprise because Omar seemed to be
their spokesperson at the beach.

She blinks at me a couple of times before turning to
Omar. "You ready?"

He nods. I wonder if he told her I was coming, but before
I can think about it too much, he touches the back of my

elbow, sending a delicious shiver up my arm. "You're cool?" he asks.

I smile. "I'm cool."

Omar and Keely are joined at the front of the room by a guy with bongo drums, a girl with a trumpet, a man who looks as old as my father with a bass guitar strapped over his shoulder, and another girl standing behind a keyboard. It's not the strangest combination of instruments I've ever seen, but the people playing them don't look like they belong together in any way.

As soon as they start playing, I know it's going to work. Keely and Omar start off with a slow, haunting duet. I try to just listen to the music, like the guy on my left with the giant red beard, who's nodding along with his beer raised. Or the girl on my other side, who's swaying along to the melody, her eyes closed.

But as they pick up speed, I can't help but look at their technique. At Keely's exquisite bowing, how her wrist never seems to stiffen up like mine does when I play in front of people. How every note that slides from her viola is perfectly in tune—effortlessly so. She's barely paying attention to her own strokes; her eyes are glued to Omar as they play.

He's looking at her, too. It's like they can't look away from each other at all. It's different from when they were on the beach. More intimate, more intense. Omar grins at her as he launches into a solo, showing off the deftness of his spiccato.

He was right. I would assume they were together if I didn't know them.

I breathe in through my nose and out through my mouth as I remind myself that he said he isn't into her like that. And that he wants to get to know me.

One by one, the other musicians join in, and the energy shifts away from Keely and Omar. But still, I watch them. I'm not sure why I'm looking when I should be listening instead. I don't know exactly what I'm looking for.

But when Omar swings his body toward where I'm standing and looks right at me, a smile lighting up his face, all my anxiety about the two of them melts away. Just for those few seconds, just when his eyes are meeting mine. That look makes me feel like I made the right choice by coming over tonight.

The guy next to me passes what I think is a joint but turns out to be a spliff. The tobacco mixed in burns the back of my throat; I take only one hit before passing it on. I close my eyes now and keep them closed as the strings take the lead again. The best way to enjoy the music is without having to watch how well Omar and Keely vibe with each other.

When they've played their last notes, the room is pulsing with energy and humid with sweat. It starts to air out a bit once people begin leaving the room, but not much. Omar stashes his violin in the case sitting in the corner and jogs over to where I'm standing by the window, trying to catch a breeze. His eyes are bright, forehead damp.

"What'd you think?"

"It was great." I fan myself with my hand. "Really great."

"Hot in here." He wipes his forehead with the back of his arm. "Want to come outside with me? I need some air."

I sneak a look at him as we walk next to each other. He has a nice profile: a strong chin and broad nose and long lashes that brush his cheeks when he blinks. I can feel the heat emanating from his body, and I hope we're alone outside. I can't stop thinking about how much I want to kiss him.

The backyard is just as sad as the front. Maybe even more so. The porch steps are crumbling at the edges, and there's an even bigger plot of grass that needs to be cut. But we are alone.

Omar touches me again, this time taking me by the hand. I hold tight as we walk across the yard to an ancient swing set that has been here long enough for the legs to rust into the ground.

"Is this safe?" I ask as he brushes leaves off the swings.

"Safe enough for sitting."

He plops down into one of the U-shaped seats. I gingerly sit next to him, holding my breath as I wait for the whole thing to come crashing down around us.

He tugs on the chains of his swing. "Promise I'm not gonna let you die on this thing."

We sway, keeping our toes planted firmly on the ground. He turns so that his legs are diagonal, his knees touching mine as he moves slowly back and forth. He dips his head to look at me.

"I'm glad you came."

"Me too." I am. But as much as I want to enjoy being alone with him right now, it's hard to forget the looks he was sharing with Keely while they played.

"Honestly, I wasn't sure it would be your kind of thing."

I turn my knees inward so they're pointing toward him, too. "What's my kind of thing?"

He tries to hide his smile. "Keely thinks you're rich."

"What?" It catches me off guard, the fact that Keely was talking about me and that he's being so open about it.

"Yeah. She said your clothes are really nice."

"She did?" I'm wearing jeans, knee-high boots, and an oversize gold sweater that falls off the shoulder. Definitely not the nicest outfit I own.

"I think she used the term *high quality*."

I shrug. "My dad makes good money, but we're not *rich* rich. Eastside comfortable, maybe."

Omar shakes his head, but he's grinning.

"What?"

"You're different from who I normally hang out with."

I stare at him. "How?"

"You know, half those people who were here tonight have trust funds waiting for them, but they'd rather die than admit that to me and my roommates. Hell, I know a couple of people who stay here have money, too. But they're weird about it. Like, they would have gone on some long rant about how they're not really rich and that it's their parents' money and blah fucking blah. You're real about what you have. It's nice."

I guess I've never felt the need to be embarrassed because my father isn't. He's honest about how much he had to sacrifice to get where he is and how much harder he has to work as a black man to succeed.

"Tonight isn't my kind of thing," I say slowly. "But it's been fun."

"I must really like you. I normally wouldn't invite someone over so soon. This place is . . . a lot for some girls."

"All the roommates?"

"The roommates, the chore chart, the way it looks outside . . . And a few of the people who live here are freegans, which means mealtime is usually interesting."

I can't help making a face.

Omar laughs. "You're not into freeganism?"

I look down at the grass, hoping he doesn't think I'm a total snob. "I guess it wouldn't be my first choice. . . ."

"Some of the stuff they bring home isn't so bad, but I stay away from anything with dairy in it. Anyway, communal living isn't for everyone, but it works for me."

He nudges my knee with his and when I look up, he kisses me. It's what I've been wanting since I first showed up, and yet I'm caught off guard. It takes a moment for me to kiss him back. I keep thinking how it's weird that he's not Warren, and it's also weird how much I'm *enjoying* that he's not Warren. I'm enjoying his lips, how they feel even better than I thought they would, firm but tender at the same time. I'm enjoying the way he leans his body closer so he can frame my knees with his on either side. I'm still holding onto the cold metal chains of the swing, and I'm glad, because when we pull away, I need something to hold me up.

He leans his forehead against mine. "Sorry . . . for surprising you like that."

"I don't think anyone needs to apologize for what just happened." I pause, but not for too long, because I don't want to lose my nerve. "Omar, do you want to go to the L.A. Phil with me? I have tickets. They're good seats. In the front orchestra."

"Eastside comfortable, huh?" he says, but he's smiling.

"They were a gift. And I want you to come with me. If, you know, you're still into that classical shit."

"Yeah. I'm still into that classical shit." He tugs lightly on one of my braids. "I'd love to go with you."

He moves his hand from my braid to my neck, gently stroking my skin with the pad of his thumb. I kiss him again, and for the first time in a long time, I feel full.

Of life, of craving, of something *new*.

And for the first time in a long time, I am happy right where I am.

14.

I haven't quite forgiven Warren for leaving me alone on my birthday, so I'm surprised to find myself back at his apartment so soon. But when he tells me his interview has been published, I drive over after school.

He didn't sound so good on the phone, and he doesn't look any better when I get there. He's pacing across his studio, from kitchen to bathroom and back again. His skin is wan, a paleness that dulls his eyes, too.

I stand by the door, watching him tread back and forth. "What's wrong?"

He points to a tall stack of *SoCal Weekly* issues centered on the coffee table. "Read it."

I take a seat on the futon and pick one up. "Warren! You're the cover story?"

He nods, biting at his fingernail.

I like the picture of him on the cover. He's standing outside my father's restaurant in his beloved chef coat, arms crossed over his chest. His mouth is set in a straight line, not frowning or smiling, and his brows are furrowed but his eyes are alive. THE NEW WONDER OF THE FOOD WORLD is emblazoned under his arms in blocky white letters.

"You look like a badass," I say, grinning, and then I'm annoyed at myself for falling back into flirting with him so easily.

I wish I could stay mad at him, the sort of anger that would let me cut off all communication and feel good about it. But as tough as I want to be when it comes to Warren, my heart is too soft.

"Yeah, and white, apparently."

"What?"

He waves his hand in the air. "Just read it."

I do. It's a well-written piece, and even though I know just about all there is to know about Warren, I read every part of the article with interest, as if he were a stranger. It doesn't dig much into his personal life, just saying he was raised in L.A. by a single mother.

"My dad gave them quotes for this?" I ask when I get to the middle. "He hates talking to reporters."

"I hope that means he won't read this, then." Across the room, Warren grimaces.

"Okay, am I missing something?" I've reached the end. I peer at the photos of him interspersed with the text. In one, he's in the kitchen, bent over as he painstakingly adds herbs to a saucepan. I guess I never realized how photogenic Warren is because he hates being in pictures. I've only seen a handful since I've known him. But even in newsprint, Warren looks good. "This is basically a perfect article."

He stops in the middle of the room and stares at me. "You didn't notice that they never mentioned I'm black?"

"Of course they did." I flip back to the beginning and skim through, paying particular attention to the paragraphs that quote or mention my father. But he's right. His or my father's race is never mentioned at all. "Did you guys talk about it during the interview?"

"I thought we did, but maybe not. I can't remember. It's all a blur, you know? I didn't even remember where we had lunch until I read the article." He puts his fingers up to his mouth again and looks down at them, disappointed when he discovers there's nothing left to bite but skin.

"It's still a good article, though. I mean, besides that, are you happy with it?"

"I don't know how I can be happy with a story that erases who I am. It's not like being black is the only interesting thing about me, but it's a big part of me. And it's not every day that someone like me comes up under someone like Sinclair. That should have been part of the story. Or they should have mentioned it, at least. Los Angeles isn't crawling with a bunch of fine-dining restaurants run by black men."

I hesitate before my next question, because I don't want to upset him even more. "Do you think she knew you were black?"

"I thought everyone knew!" He sighs, and it looks like his whole body is deflating. "Or at least someone who's writing a cover story about me."

He walks to the counter that separates the kitchen from the main room and plops his elbows down, resting his head in his hands. I don't think I've ever seen Warren upset like this. I don't like it.

I place the paper back on the table and walk across the room. I stand behind him for a couple of moments before I slip my arms around his middle and press my cheek to his back. "I'm sorry, Warren. But maybe this is just the beginning. Someone could be reading this right now, wondering why they didn't mention you're black. Maybe another writer, who can do another story on you."

"I'm not that big, Yvonne," he says, his voice low.

I don't realize that I'm counting the beats of my heart against his back until he takes my hands and turns around to face me. He rubs his thumb over my cheekbone, and when I look up into his eyes, I know he's going to kiss me.

There's an insistence behind his kiss that I've never felt before. Like he'll lose me forever if our lips part. Kissing Warren is safe and familiar, and I guess maybe that's why I don't stop. I can't be mad at him anymore. Warren feels like home.

We end up on his bed, sitting at first. He kisses every inch of skin from my chin to my collarbone, and I want to melt right into him. I wonder if I should tell him about Omar; I've never mentioned any of the other guys I've kissed, but Omar seems different. Like maybe he's going to be around for a while.

"What's wrong?" Warren asks, sensing my hesitation.

"Nothing." I tug on the hem of his shirt. He smiles and raises his arms so I can pull it over his head.

He undresses me until I'm wearing only my underwear. His hands trail slowly down to caress my shoulders, my breasts, my waist. When he gets to my hips, he hooks his thumbs on either side of my underwear and slides them slowly over my thighs. I look at him for a long moment, both shy and expectant, before I lie back.

I feel his breath, warm between my legs, and then Warren's mouth is on me. It feels wonderful and strange all at once. New for us. I stare at the ceiling, and then, once I'm used to the rhythm and touch, I close my eyes. Warren's hands slide up and down my legs, and my whole body is warm and I'm breathing so fast, I wonder if I'm hyperventilating. But then my legs tighten and I murmur his name and squeeze his shoulders, and the most pleasurable feeling rolls through me in waves.

He slowly eases off, kissing my thighs as he pulls away. I close my eyes again to get my bearings. When I open them, Warren is lying next to me. He stretches my arm over his chest, stroking the inside.

"That wasn't the first time you got off?"

"No. Well, the first time from someone besides myself," I say, looking at my arm instead of him.

"Ahh." I can hear the smile in his voice but also the apprehension. "You liked it?"

"Obviously." I flick his arm and he leans over to kiss my shoulder.

Again, I wonder if I should bring up the fact that I've started seeing someone else. But it's not like Warren and I had actual sex. And Omar and I haven't even gone this far. I don't want to get too ahead of myself or upset Warren for nothing. He knows I've been with other guys, but now that my age is no longer a factor for him, it feels different between us. Like every moment is filled with more meaning because it could lead to something real.

I don't want to ruin the moment. As much as I've tried to distance myself from Warren since my birthday, I still care about him, and what just happened between us was special. Something I'll remember forever.

"Warren?"

"Hmm?"

I don't know what I want to say. He doesn't ask me about it. I curl into him, and he lightly rubs my back, and we lie together in his apartment, bathed in the early evening light.

15.

Lemon meringue pie has never been one of my favorite desserts, but I like it—the tanginess of the lemons paired with the sweetness of the tall, fluffy meringue. The pies always catch my eye in pastry cases, yet I can't say I've ever thought of making one. The meringue looks so precarious, and I know from watching enough baking shows that it can be difficult to perfect.

Lou didn't give me any pointers, so by the time I get up on Saturday, ready to bake, I've read through the recipe in my mother's cookbook and looked over a few more online. Still, I carry the book under one arm and my laptop in the other as I head to the kitchen.

I put on a pot of coffee and open the book. The page

is free of my mother's scribbles, so this must not have been a recipe she made often. I'm oddly comforted. Sometimes looking at her handwriting brings up too many feelings.

I pull out all the ingredients for the crust, but I don't get started until I'm halfway through my first cup of coffee. I never realized how therapeutic making pie dough could be. I love the way it feels to work my fingers through it and how I can get lost in the task, forgetting about everything taking up space in my head. I used to feel that way about violin, when I was younger. I could lose myself in the emotions of the piece rather than focusing so much on the technicalities of playing.

Dad stumbles into the kitchen moments after I slide the pie dough into the oven. He nods hello, heading straight to the coffee maker.

"Next assignment for Lou?" he asks after a couple of sips.

"Yeah." I'm cleaning up so I'll have less to do after I make the pie filling. "He's coming over for dessert tomorrow, remember?"

"I remember." Dad peers at the cookbook. "Huh. That meringue can be a real bitch."

"So I've heard."

He takes his coffee out to the sunroom, and today I follow him, making sure the timer is set on my phone for the piecrust. He looks up as I walk in, frowning.

"Need something?"

"No. It's been a while since I was in here."

He shrugs as if it's okay, but I know he doesn't like me being in the sunroom. It's become his dominion, a more cultured version of the man cave. He doesn't watch TV—not even sports—so there's no television set in here. It looks more like an old den or a study, except it doesn't have that dark, mahogany-wood-and-cigars look because sun pours in through the two full walls of windows most of the day.

He sits on the love seat, and I flop down onto the chaise, watching him pull out his weed box. It's a nice wooden box with a gold clasp that I guess other people would use for keepsakes. It's quite organized inside: the actual weed—or flowers, as he calls it—on the left side, a couple of Bic lighters on the top right, and his preferred pipes below those. I watch him crumble the herb onto the flipped-over top of the box, then pinch it methodically into the bowl of his pipe.

"What?" he says, the pipe in one hand, a white lighter hovering in the other.

"I didn't say anything."

My father sighs. "You're watching me."

"I'm just sitting here."

He shakes his head and lifts the pipe to his mouth, taking a long hit. He exhales away from me, the smoke pouring out in a slow, billowing stream. "You know, sometimes I wonder if you're judging me."

"You're aware that I've smoked before, right?" I decide to phrase it that way, rather than the present tense.

"You're a teenager living in L.A.," he says drily. "I'm aware."

"Well, then I can't really judge you. And I didn't think you cared what other people thought, anyway."

"Why would you think that?"

"Because that's how you act?"

He looks thoughtfully at his pipe. "It's not an issue in my industry—it's the people on the outside. I don't want to seem like I'm perpetuating a stereotype of a black man. I shouldn't have to explain myself to anyone when I'm getting along just fine."

"But it doesn't really matter what those people think, right? They're wrong for judging you."

"They may be wrong, but it's my reputation on the line. I want to be known for my food, not my personal choices."

I nod. He's always been so aware of appearances, this doesn't surprise me. Even back when we had our two-second talk about sex, I got the idea that he was more concerned about me preventing pregnancy than diseases when he told me to use protection.

"Why do you like it out here so much?"

He flicks the lighter on again, passing it over the top of the bowl. He takes a moment after he exhales to look around the room—at his bookshelf of chef memoirs, the side table where he stores his laptop, the chess set gathering dust on the coffee table between us. "It's comfortable out here. My own space."

"Did you come out here when Mom was still around?"

He coughs so much I'd think his lungs were still filled with smoke if it weren't all floating in the air above us. "Why are you so full of questions today?" His voice isn't unkind, but he sounds genuinely surprised.

"You don't tell me anything unless I ask."

"This was your mom's room. . . . You don't remember?"

Not at all. For as long as I've known, this room has been my father's. I remember being around her all the time, but never here.

"What did she do out here?"

He's silent for too long.

The timer on my phone dings.

I stand, but before I go to the kitchen, I look back at him.

"I don't know, Yvonne," he finally says. "I wish I did."

Meringue *is* a bit of a bitch.

The first one I made collapsed, and I had to start over. The second one came out perfect, and I'm even proud of the way I was able to brown the peaks on top.

"Looks beautiful," Lou says the next day, carefully turning the pie so he can admire it from all angles.

It does look nice, but when he cuts into it, there's a layer of liquid between the meringue and the filling. I sigh and look at him.

"It's okay," he says, sliding a piece onto my plate first, then my father's and then his. "It's called weeping. Happens all the time. Was the filling hot when you layered on the meringue?"

I can't remember. I was so exhausted by the time I finally got the meringue right that I stopped paying attention to all the little details I'd read about before I started.

"If you make sure the filling is hot, the meringue will cook all the way through and won't weep," he offers.

I nod and hold my breath, and both Dad and I watch as he takes the first bite.

Lou chews thoughtfully. Slides in another forkful and swallows before he looks at me. "This is an objectively good attempt at your first lemon meringue pie, Yvonne."

But.

"It tastes great and I'm impressed with your meringue. This was the first time you've made it?"

Across the table, my father finally bites into his piece, as if he needed Lou's approval before he dug in. It hurts my feelings, but I try to ignore it and focus on Lou.

"Yeah. The one you're looking at is my second try, but this is my first time making it."

"My other critique is the crust," he continues. "It should be flaky, but this is a little tough. Almost chewy. That usually means the butter you used wasn't cold enough or you didn't let the dough chill long enough before you put it into the oven."

I think back to yesterday, when I set out all the ingredients first—including the butter. *Then* I had my coffee. I push my plate away.

"Don't be so hard on yourself." Lou smiles. "This is nothing to be embarrassed about. Right, Sinclair?"

My father nods. "It's a noble effort."

"Your father presented me with some less than impressive dishes when he was starting out," Lou says. "It comes with the territory. Cooking isn't easy, and baking is even more precise."

I am embarrassed, though. I didn't think I was a baking prodigy, but it felt right—up until this point. Like maybe it would give me something to focus on besides violin. An activity I like and feel good about—something to occupy my time.

"I want you to try this again," Lou says after he's finished his whole piece. My father cleans his plate, too, but neither of them goes back for seconds. "And then, when we're satisfied with this, we'll move on to something else. People think pastry chefs have it easy, but I thank my lucky stars for mine each day. She's not perfect, but she works her butt off to make sure it looks like she is. It's all about practice and knowledge."

Practice and knowledge didn't serve me so well when it came to violin, even after all the years I've spent with it, also striving for perfectionism. What if Lou is wrong? What if I'm only good at baking a couple of things and I'm wasting everyone's time? Maybe it's exciting now because it's something new, but I'll eventually grow bored or frustrated with it.

I wait until they're caught up in a heated discussion about a new restaurant in West Hollywood before I taste the pie. Lou is right about everything. The pie is too wet and the crust too dense. One bite is all I need.

I pretend that I'm clearing the table to be helpful, but on my second trip to the kitchen, I bring the rest of the pie and throw it into the garbage.

16.

"So, where are you applying?"

It's the question I've been wanting to avoid since my talk with Ortiz, but Kama Hobart finally asks. As soon as I sit down in orchestra on Monday. She's genuinely sweet and one of the least competitive people in the orchestra. But she's also very, very good.

"Oh, I'm not sure. I'm a little behind," I say with a faux-sheepish look as I snap open my case. I guess I should come up with a better answer than that, but I'm still staunchly avoiding my applications. "What about you?"

Kama runs a hand through her red curls, looking toward the ceiling as she thinks. "Northwestern, USC, Rice, Michigan, and Curtis...I think that's it."

"Wait—you're not only applying to conservatories?"

She laughs. "Are you kidding? Curtis is a long shot, but I couldn't *not* apply. It's my dream school."

"But you'll totally get into all those others." I remove my bow and rosin. "You'll probably get into Curtis, too."

"That's sweet of you, Yvonne, but it's not true. It's competitive as shit out there. I just started doing real competitions our freshman year. Some people have been at it since elementary."

I sweep my bow through the rosin. She sounds like Denis. Or maybe like any rational person who's been playing violin as long as we have. I never did any of those competitions. Denis and I talked about it—or rather, he hinted many times that I would have to advance beyond the local contests if I wanted to keep working with him—but I never liked competing. There was so much pressure, so many people watching. And the thought of being judged and rated always seemed so cruel. Maybe that should have been my first sign that I wasn't cut out for this.

Ortiz comes in then, and I'm relieved because I don't want to talk about this with Kama. As we warm up, I wonder if she can hear a difference in how I play now. I never feel like I'm quite in tune anymore, and my fingers are slow and heavy on the bow. I'd be surprised if anyone hasn't noticed the change. But everyone is either too caught up in their own playing or too nice to say anything.

In addition to practicing for the holiday program, we're working on a Haydn concerto because Ortiz is obsessed with Haydn.

I try to talk myself into putting energy behind it, into pushing myself to make my violin sing. I've done it before—I should be able to do it again if I really concentrate. I think of Omar and Keely the other night, how free they were but also how utterly engaged. How I could practically see the passion flowing through their veins. It was magical. This feels methodical. Boring.

We're all packing up our things when Ms. Ortiz says, "Come see me before you leave, Yvonne?"

I nod, but I can feel Ortiz watching, as if she thinks I'm going to bail before she gets a chance to talk to me. Once the last person has exited the room, I walk up to the front, bag and violin hooked over my shoulders.

"Am I in trouble?"

Ortiz presses her lips together as she looks at me. "This time? Maybe. What's going on with you?"

"What do you mean?"

"Ever since our talk, it's like you've been replaced with a robot. It's like *all* your fire is gone."

"I just feel...confused now. I wonder if I should even be playing."

"Haydn?"

"All of it. It doesn't feel right."

She studies me. "Do you still like the violin?"

I nod.

"What do you like about it?"

"I don't know.... It's just something I've done forever."

"That's not a good reason," she says, shaking her head. "That's when people get into trouble, doing something just because it's what they've always done."

"I do like it." I pause. I don't want to admit that I'm afraid the loneliness would crush me if I gave it up altogether. "What about other careers in music?"

"Well, there's teaching. Of course, you'd still have to be present and dedicated. Maybe even more so, because you'd be shaping young minds."

I wrinkle my nose. "No offense, but I don't think teaching is for me."

"None taken," she says with a laugh. "It wasn't the path I would have chosen for myself in high school."

"What did you want to do?"

Ortiz raises her eyebrows. "You really want to hear about this?"

"I need all the help I can get."

"Well, after I graduated from Berklee, I started auditioning for symphonies. I was willing to move almost anywhere that would let me play. I ended up in Iowa and became a section leader. It was fine for a while, but I wanted to be a conductor."

Now it's my turn to raise my eyebrows. I never would have guessed Ortiz didn't want to teach. She's so good at what she does; she always seems so happy.

"And I quickly found out that conducting was thought to be a man's world. I couldn't break in. Or maybe I should say I wasn't willing to wait around and luck into an opportunity. I wasn't happy in the orchestra, so I started teaching."

"Did you ever consider anything else?"

"Consider, yes. I thought about trying almost everything, but I knew this was my best option to keep working in music. And there are more paths to take than teaching. You could try a music therapy program. I've had a few students go on to do that, and they find it so fulfilling."

I knew music therapy existed, but it never seemed like something people actually went to school to do.

"And there are fields where you could combine other talents with your background. Like being a music critic or an orchestra manager. You could get into public relations for a symphony.... There's so much you can do with the training you've had up to this point."

None of those careers ever occurred to me, and while they sound appealing enough in general, nothing stands out.

"The bell's about to ring, but please come see me with any more questions," Ortiz says with a warm smile. "I'm happy to see you thinking about your choices, Yvonne. You're a smart girl. You can go far, whatever you do."

When I get home from school, Warren is waiting for me.

He stands up from his seat on the front steps and brushes his hands on the front of his jeans as I approach.

"Hey," I say, stopping in front of him. "What's going on?"

"How was your day?" I hate when people answer a question with a question. It never means they have anything good to say.

"It was fine. Warren, what's wrong?"

"I need to talk to you." His voice is strained, and that's when I notice he doesn't look much better than the last time I saw him, the day the article was published. Dark bags have settled in below his eyes, and his posture is awful, like he can barely hold himself up.

"Let's go inside."

I leave my violin and bag by the front door and lead Warren to the couch. I don't press him to say anything once we're sitting. He takes a couple of deep breaths.

"Do you want water? Tea?" I offer, thinking maybe that will help him get the words out.

"No. My..." His voice comes out thin. He clears his throat and starts over. "My dad emailed me."

"Oh my God, Warren. What did he say?"

Warren twists his hands together so hard it makes me cringe. "He saw the article and now he wants to see me."

"What are you going to do?"

"I don't know." He looks at me. "What would you do? If your mom showed up out of nowhere and wanted to meet up with you?"

I've thought about this, of course. Maybe a million times.

And I still don't have an answer. Part of me would want to see her immediately, if only to confirm that she was real and not just a name linked to a collection of old, useless things and fragmented memories. But the other part would ignore her forever, wanting to punish her for leaving me without a mother and full of endless questions about why she left.

"Yvonne?" he prompts me when I take too long to respond.

"I'd probably want to see her," I say softly.

"But you remember your mom. He took off when I was *two*."

"What does he do now?" I ask, wrapping Warren's hands in mine. They're cold and clammy, but it makes him stop wringing them and he seems to appreciate the comfort.

"I don't know. He didn't say anything about himself. Just that he lives in the area and wants to see me. More like *meet* me. Why couldn't he just come to the restaurant and spy on me?"

"I don't know, War. But I think this might be good." His hands are slowly warming up in mine. "If he just came in and didn't say anything, you'd never have to know he wanted to see you. It's cowardly. This way, he doesn't get to be let off the hook."

"Yeah...I guess you're right."

"Of course I'm right."

The corner of his mouth briefly turns up in a half-smile,

then fades. "I was also wondering... or hoping... if I do this, will you come with me? When I meet him? I don't think I'm going to tell my mom. No need to put her through that, you know?"

I can't imagine not telling my father I was going to meet my mother, but it's different with Warren. He doesn't live with his mom anymore, and she's remarried now. He once said she hadn't mentioned his father in years.

"I'll come with you." I squeeze his hand. "Just let me know when."

I wonder again if I should tell him about Omar. We're going to the L.A. Philharmonic in just a few days. I don't think Warren will care that I'm not taking him, but he will care that I'm using the extra ticket on a guy I can't seem to stop thinking about. A guy that I think I could care about.

It doesn't feel like the right time. He's relieved that I'm going with him to meet his dad—that much is clear—but he's still visibly rattled. I can't kick him when he's down. Not like this.

"I know I don't deserve you," he says after a long pause. "But thank you."

He leans his head against my shoulder, and I wrap my arms around him, pulling him close.

17.

The Walt Disney Concert Hall is one of the most beautiful buildings in Los Angeles, the kind you stop to stare at every time you drive or walk by, no matter how many times you've seen it.

I am running late the night of the L.A. Phil performance, so I call a car and do my makeup on the way over. It's a relief not to have to deal with driving downtown and parking in the garage, which is always a clusterfuck the evening of an event.

Omar is waiting for me out front. He seemed embarrassed when he told me he didn't have a car and would have to take the subway, but I don't mind meeting him here. It gives me more time to get my nerves in check. I guess the evening at his house was our first date, but this feels more like a real one. Just the two of us, all dressed up.

"You look gorgeous," he says, kissing my cheek.

I wanted him to greet me with a kiss on the lips, but maybe we're not there yet. And he called me gorgeous, which makes my neck flush with heat.

I decided on the blue dress. No one saw me in it on my birthday except Sabina and Warren, and nothing else felt right for this evening. Now, seeing the way Omar is looking at me, I'm glad I wore it.

"You look nice, too."

His locs are pulled back again, and he's wearing a blue button-down shirt and gray dress pants. I've never seen him in anything so nice, and I like it. He smiles and takes my hand. "Ready to go in?"

I've heard that people in Los Angeles don't dress up like they do in New York, but you couldn't tell from this crowd. The terrace and lobby are bustling with crisp suits and glittering dresses that probably cost more than every piece of clothing I own.

"They go all out here, huh?" Omar looks down at his outfit. "Should I have worn a jacket?"

"You're fine." I loop my arm through his as we walk. "That guy isn't wearing a jacket.... Neither is he...."

I point out enough jacketless guys that Omar relaxes.

"It's been a while since I've been to one of these things," he says. "Never been to the L.A. Phil."

"I went last year, with some people from my orchestra."

"Oh, yeah? How's that going?"

"Okay, I guess.... I talked to my teacher about ways to have music that don't involve performing. I'm thinking about quitting, but I can't bring myself to do it."

"Why not?"

I bite my lip before I speak. "Do you feel attached to your violin?"

"Yeah, of course."

I hesitate because I'm so afraid of sounding immature or pathetic, but if I can't talk to Omar about this, who *can* I talk to? "I mean, *really* attached. Like, it would feel as if you lost someone close to you if you set it down forever?"

I look down at my shoes, afraid that he'll mock me for sounding like a little girl who doesn't want to give up her stuffed animals. But when I look up, he's considering my question, not dismissing it. "I never thought about it like that. For me, it's more about the music. About playing. If I lost a finger or a hand, it would be tragic for the obvious reasons, but I'd kind of feel like what's the point of even having a violin if I can't play?"

"I wish I felt like that." I look up at the sky, where the sun has almost finished setting, making room for the moon.

"How you feel is fine, Yvonne." His fingers find my hand at my side. He gently strokes my wrist. "Sometimes it takes a while to figure out what you want. No one could've told me I would've dropped out of Berklee and been happy today."

154

"You don't regret it?"

"Not for a minute." And then, as if he knows I needed it, he kisses me on the lips. It's swift but sweet. When I open my eyes, he's looking at me. "You have to trust yourself. Do what's right for you, no matter what anyone else says."

I wish I could do that, but after talking to my dad, who I thought was the most confident person in the world, shutting out other people's opinions seems easier said than done.

Our seats are really good, and I want to text Warren to thank him, but I'll have to wait until later. Omar is never on his phone—always attentive and present. Which is new; not what I'm used to from hanging out with guys my age. He's not that much older—he's twenty, a year younger than Warren. But he reads older. Like an old soul.

"I love this feeling, before it begins."

I don't realize I've said it out loud until Omar looks over and smiles. "What do you like about it?"

I feel shy now, but I make myself talk. "It's, like, a feeling in the air...like everyone knows something special is going to happen. And I like watching the orchestra get ready. I love hearing them tune up and wondering how important the performance is to all of them...who it means more to."

He looks around for a minute, then leans in. "Do you ever feel weird at things like this? Being around all this money?"

"It can be a lot," I say, though it doesn't weird me out. This city is full of rich people who don't look rich; it's always interesting to be around the ones who have no problem flaunting their wealth.

Tonight, the orchestra is playing pieces from *Romeo and Juliet*, selections adapted from the ballet composed by Prokofiev. I don't think there's any way Warren could have known this, but the orchestral suites contain some of my favorite classical work.

I lean forward through the whole suite, closing my eyes when the strings are front and center, imagining myself onstage. Ortiz has never had us play Prokofiev, but Denis assigned me some pieces to work on, and the "Montagues and Capulets" was one of them. It is so authoritative and determined and beautiful, I always felt powerful when I practiced. Playing it was one of the few times I really lost myself in the music and came out of it at the end staring at Denis confused, as if someone else had taken over my body.

There's no intermission, and I'm glad because I prefer watching the program without taking breaks. I glance at Omar a couple of times, hoping he's not bored. He looks enthralled, his eyes dancing across the stage as he takes in the performance. The second time I catch his eye, he smiles and takes my hand, resting them both on his knee. It's hard for me to focus on the music after that, because I feel so good sitting like this with Omar, my hand enveloped in his.

The orchestra receives a well-deserved standing ovation, and when it's all over, I sink back into my seat with a sigh.

"What'd you think?" Omar asks.

"I loved it. Everything about it."

"I was kinda worried about coming to this," he says. "I thought I might miss this life...or what could've been my life. But I don't. I feel like I'm doing what I was supposed to do, even if it's tough, you know?"

I nod, even though I don't know. I haven't found that yet. And it scares me.

Outside, we stand again in front of the concert hall, watching people stream out to waiting cars and take pictures in front of the building. The moon is out, its natural light competing with the aggressive street lamps of Grand Avenue.

"So...what should we do now?" It's sort of bold and definitely presumptuous to assume he still wants to hang out, but we spent the evening next to each other, not talking at all. I don't want the night to be over yet.

"Even though it's a school night?"

"I don't have a curfew." But I don't think that's the issue. Especially when I see the uncomfortable look that flickers across his face.

Omar has never said he's broke, but all signs add up to that. I can't imagine he makes a lot at the youth center.

"I have to tell you something," he says, "and I don't mean for it to be a big deal, but I think you should know."

"Okay...."

"I told you Keely and I are roommates, but we actually share a room at the house. Not a bed," he adds quickly, and I'm not sure that makes me feel any better.

The whole thing makes me feel a little sick, actually. How can you just share a room with someone you used to care about and sleep with and then pretend like everything is normal?

"I hope that doesn't change anything between us." He steps closer and tilts his head to the side as he looks at me. "I really like you, Yvonne. I thought the high school thing would be weird, but it's not. You don't act young."

"I'm not *that* young. I'm eighteen."

"I know." He clears his throat. "Anyway, I want to ask you back to my place, but I can't. Not unless we want to hang out on the swing set all night. I'm sorry."

He does sound sorry, which makes me think maybe his feelings for Keely have truly faded. Omar seems like an honest guy. He's shown me where he lives—it doesn't get much more personal than that.

"I don't know what to say."

"I get it. And I'll understand if you don't want to keep seeing me, but—"

"That's not what I mean. It's just...something I haven't dealt with before, I guess. I don't want to stop seeing you."

He exhales slowly. "That makes me happy, Yvonne."

"Are you hungry?" I ask after a few moments. "We could grab some food and go back to my house."

"Your parents won't care?"

"My dad works late. He won't be home for a while."

"If you're sure..."

"I'm positive. I know a great place where we can get takeout."

I call a car and on the way over, I read the menu to Omar, and we choose a few items to share. I call in the order, telling the host who I am right away, because technically my father's restaurant doesn't do takeout. It's the middle of the week, so it's probably not too busy for us to snag a table, but I'm sure Warren is working. And I don't want to have to explain to my father who Omar is. I haven't exactly mentioned I'm seeing someone.

"I'll be right back," I say when we get to the restaurant, jumping out before Omar can offer to come with me.

The restaurant is busier than I figured, so I think maybe I'll get in and out without having to see my father or Warren. But when the host comes back with the bags of food, he's accompanied by Warren, who is sweaty from the kitchen but looks a little less anxious than the last time I saw him. A little.

"Thanks, Frank." I take the bags from him, then walk a few feet away with Warren. "What's up?"

"What's up with *you*?" he says, gesturing to my dress.

"Oh. The L.A. Phil."

"That was tonight?"

"Yeah, I—you said I didn't have to take you."

"I know. And I meant that. How was it?"

"It was perfect. The seats, the music, everything. Thank you."

He smiles. "It's the least I could do. But don't tell me you're eating all that yourself?"

"No, it's—Sabina's waiting in the car, but we didn't feel like eating here." I hate lying to Warren.

"Well, I'm glad you stopped by. I wanted to tell you that I emailed him back today. My dad."

"And...?"

"And he wants to meet this weekend. Sunday brunch. He said I can pick the place. You're still down to come with me?"

"Warren, of course." His eyes are so scared and unsure that I have to resist the urge to reach up and cup his face in my hand. "I wouldn't miss it."

He looks like he wants to kiss me, so I give him a quick hug and say I have to go, practically sprinting out the door and into the waiting car.

18.

"Nice house," Omar says as we walk from the front door to the kitchen. "Just you and your parents?"

"Just me and my dad. My mom isn't around."

"Oh." He stops there, but I can tell there's more he wants to say.

"That was a loaded *oh*." I grab plates from the cabinet and bring them back to the table.

"Okay, promise you won't think I'm an asshole for saying this, but you don't really seem like the sort of person whose parent just wouldn't be around."

"Well, I am. She disappeared when I was six."

He helps me unload the food from the containers: butter

lettuce salad, calamari, lobster Bolognese, roasted sea bass, and a sampling of fresh bread. Omar's eyes widen.

"I guess I didn't realize how much food we got. This is... a lot. Let me know how much I owe you."

"You don't owe me anything. My dad owns the restaurant."

"What?"

"Yeah. They don't really do takeout."

"We don't see a lot of food like this at the house," he says. "Guess they're hitting up the wrong alleys."

"They wouldn't find anything there." I sit down with my plate full of food. "He donates anything left over to a food rescue program that feeds the homeless."

"Sounds like a good guy," Omar says, taking the seat across from me. He spreads a napkin over his lap.

"He's all right."

"Just all right?"

"I don't really know him."

"He's your dad."

"Exactly. He doesn't reveal a lot about himself. I never know what he's thinking or feeling. Sometimes it's more like we're roommates."

"That sounds frustrating."

"Yeah." I pause. "So... why did you say I don't seem like the type of person whose mom wouldn't be around?"

He twirls a bite of pasta onto his fork and chews, thinking. "Well," he says after he swallows, "for starters, your dad owns a restaurant that serves lobster Bolognese. I've never even heard of lobster Bolognese."

"Okay...what else?"

"I don't notice clothes much, but I can tell that your house is full of nice things," he says. "The art and furniture look expensive.... You've got books everywhere.... Even the rug looks pretty fancy."

I'm aware that we have a nice place, but it's so modest compared with so many of my classmates that I never thought anyone would be this impressed. It's not a big house, and among the Courtland Academy families, bigger usually means better. Then again, probably anything looks nicer than Omar's place, with the deteriorating exterior and refrigerators in the dining room.

"If it makes you feel any better, my dad is a total stoner who pretty much stays high all the time so he doesn't have to access his emotions."

"Whoa," Omar says, holding a piece of bread in midair. "That sounded pretty clinical."

"My best friend figured it out for me," I say. "One of her moms is a therapist."

"You cool with him smoking?"

"Yeah...I guess." I don't tell Omar that I rarely invite new people over precisely because I don't want them judging my father. I'm not always sure how I feel about him myself, but I don't need anyone else's opinion.

"You know," Omar says slowly, and my whole body tenses because I wonder if he's going to drop another bomb about him and Keely. He pauses, then stops.

"Yeah?"

"Keely and I . . ."

Oh, Jesus.

". . . we were on the streets for a while."

My mouth drops open. "Like, actually homeless?"

"Like, actually homeless. We stayed in a few shelters, but Keely was too skeeved out and couldn't sleep, so we went off on our own. We set up in a camp under a 101 overpass for a while, then we kept moving west until we heard about an open room in the house. Been there ever since."

"Wow. I had no idea. How long?"

"About three months, I think. Hard to track time when you're moving around like that."

"So, what—I mean, how—" I can't think of an eloquent way to ask my question.

"How did we end up homeless? I'd dropped out of Berklee and spent all my money traveling. Keely was in a bad situation at home with her piece-of-shit dad, and once she met me she felt like she could finally leave. But we didn't have any place to go. The only things we had worth selling were our instruments, and that was the only way we knew how to make money." He lowers his head. "I'm not proud of it, but I'm proud we got out of it."

164

"You have nothing to be ashamed of." I touch his arm. "All my money comes from my dad. I wouldn't know what to do if things were awful with him."

Of course I could call on Sabina or Warren or Lou, or even people I don't know all that well at Courtland. They wouldn't let me live on the streets, and it makes me sad to think that Keely didn't have anyone she could go to.

Omar flips his hand over, palm up, and catches my hand in his.

When we're finished eating, he asks to see my violin.

"Oh, it's not that nice," I say. "It's no Stradivarius, if that's what you're expecting."

"With you, I wouldn't be surprised," he says, but he's smiling. "I want to see it anyway."

I lead him back to my room, heart thumping under the lace of my dress. No guy has ever been in my room but Warren. I feel a little strange about it, but my excitement about getting to kiss Omar again trumps any of my reservations.

I retrieve my violin case and snap it open. On the other side of the bed, Omar leans over to peer at it, fingers running across the smooth wood.

"Looks like a pretty nice fiddle to me. Better than some I saw at Berklee."

"Really?" Denis always looked at it disdainfully, as if it were beneath him to work with a student who wasn't toting around a million-dollar instrument.

"It's not cheap," Omar says. "I'd love to hear what it sounds like."

"Be my guest." I nod toward the case.

He laughs. "Nice try. I want to hear what *you* sound like."

"I don't think you do."

"Come on, Yvonne," he says softly. "I was watching you tonight. You still love it. Nobody looks that way if they don't love it."

I stare at my violin like I've never seen it, like it's not something I've carried with me almost every day for the past eleven years. I've never treated anything so carefully, never owned anything so fragile that was part of my everyday life.

"I do love it. It's just...I've heard you play. You're so much better than me."

"Good, better... it's all subjective."

He's not going to let me get out of this unless I kick him out, and that's not happening. I pick up the violin and bow as slowly as I can, stalling while I think of what to play. I wish I knew something contemporary, but Ortiz doesn't let us play around much, and Denis certainly stuck to classical. I can't play the "Montagues and Capulets" because we just heard such a stunning rendition, and I'd never do it justice.

I settle on a movement from a Vivaldi concerto, the one I played for Ortiz. It's not the most difficult piece I know, but maybe that means I'll have fewer opportunities to mess this up. I'm a little rusty at first—there's no denying that. I don't look at Omar's face to see if he noticed because of course he noticed. He plays every single day. I think of all the times I skipped practicing or rushed through it, and I wonder if I'd be prepping for conservatory auditions if only I'd tried harder. If I'd listened to Denis more than I scoffed at him behind his back.

My bow hits a sour note.

I pull the violin down from my chin, ready to make an excuse, but Omar shakes his head and stares at me until I start again.

I try to think of something—anything—that will soothe my nerves, but I just keep thinking how odd it is that I'm standing here in my mother's dress, playing violin for a guy I'm still getting to know. And then I think of my mother. Did she leave this dress for me, knowing I'd want to wear it someday? What would she think of me now, if she could see me? Why has she never tried to contact me, like Warren's dad contacted him? I get angrier and angrier, and that ferocity comes through as my bow glides rapidly across the strings.

When I stop, I am drained. I set my violin on my desk and look at Omar, almost with defiance. Daring him to tell me I should be applying to conservatories.

He doesn't.

But he does walk around the bed and slip his arms around my waist, and he never once looks away from me.

"Do you still think good is subjective?" I ask.

"Yes," he says. "But for the record, I think you *are* good. That was a damn good Vivaldi."

"Yeah?" I look at him shyly, my bashfulness starting to fade.

He answers me with a kiss. And then another. He kisses me so deeply again and again that I feel dizzy when we pull away.

"I liked you from the first time I saw you," he murmurs, his hands sliding up and down my lace-covered hips. "But I thought you were too young."

"Would you stop it with the 'young' thing?" I playfully tweak one of his locs.

"Okay, I also thought that guy was your boyfriend."

"What guy—" Oh. I forgot that Warren was with me the first time I talked to Omar. Omar, who is tall enough that I have to stand on my tiptoes to brush my lips against his neck. "He's not my boyfriend."

I feel guilty for a moment, denying Warren like that. But it's true. And then Omar backs me up until I'm pressed against the wall, and I forget about Warren because we're kissing again. Omar's hands cup my ass and then one travels under my dress, running over the lace on my panties, too. He finds the zipper on the back of my dress and sends it dashing down my spine. The air is cool on my back and then the rest of me as he slides the dress from my shoulders.

"Wait," he says, as I'm unbuttoning his shirt. I don't stop, but I look up so he'll know I'm listening. "Is your dad gonna come home and kick my ass for being here?"

I glance at the clock on my wall. "He won't be home for at least a couple more hours. We're fine."

And soon, we're in my bed. Time feels like it truly stops when I'm kissing Omar. I don't know how to explain it, but I feel freer with him than I've ever felt with anyone—even Warren. Maybe it's because he touches me so freely, without hesitation. His hands are slow and gentle, but I'm very much aware that he knows what he's doing. That feeling in the air between us—that spark I felt the first day I talked to him— moves to my body. It crackles through my veins and along my skin. I am electric under his touch.

I don't know if it's the high from the performance or that I let myself go enough to play for him, but I feel like I'm floating. And when we're in that delicate space, the pause between sex and no sex, I don't hesitate long.

I say yes—with my hands, with my hips, with my mouth. I give him all of me.

19.

I love Sabina for many reasons, and the fact that she helps me take down my box braids is high on the list. I can do it myself, but it's faster when I have two extra hands— and always more fun when Sabina is around.

She comes over Friday night, a couple of days after my date with Omar, armed with a large bag of Swedish Fish, salt and vinegar chips, and chocolate-covered pretzels.

"Running out of snacks makes me nervous," she says when I remind her that a pizza is on the way.

After it arrives, I set the box on the kitchen table while I grab plates and napkins. Sabina starts to sit down, but I look over my shoulder and say, "I thought we could eat in the sunroom."

When I turn around, she's frowning. "Your dad's weed room?"

"It's not *just* his weed room. It's kind of nice in there."

She scrunches her nose but obliges. We inhale the first slices of pizza without talking. It's from our favorite place, and we always get the same kind: prosciutto and arugula, which Sabina deemed the most bougie pizza that ever existed until she tried it and fell in love.

"It's not so bad in here. It doesn't reek of weed, anyway," Sabina says, taking a break after the first piece. "But is there a reason we're in here?"

"I don't know. I never hang out in here...."

"Honestly, I didn't think you were *allowed* in here." She looks around with her eyes narrowed as if she expects my father to jump out of hiding and reprimand us.

"It's not off-limits," I say, though I'm certain my father wouldn't be too excited by the idea of my best friend scarfing pizza on his love seat.

"Are you trying to, like, figure out your dad or something?"

"My mom."

She pulls another slice of pizza from the pie. "I don't get it."

"Dad said she used to hang out in here...but he doesn't know why. And I don't remember her spending time in this room, which is bugging the shit out of me."

"So you think you'll get some special feeling that'll make you figure out why she left?"

"No—yes—I don't know. It can't hurt, right?"

We lie around complaining about how much pizza we ate, then clean up and move to my room. Sabina sits on the bed and starts on the back of my head, unraveling the tight plaits from the bottom up, while I work on the ones at the front from my cross-legged position on the floor.

"Has that guy from the beach asked you out again?" She drops a strand of the added hair into the paper bag by my side.

I push my fingers into the loose, soft strands of hair at my neck that she uncovered, feeling it for the first time in weeks. "Not yet, but he called the day after our date to say how much fun he had."

"I can't believe you guys talk on the phone."

"Yeah, it's weird. Even Warren and I text more often than not. He seems old-fashioned like that... a gentleman."

"*Gentleman?* Wow." She pauses, her fingers working quickly at the back of my head. "All that stuff about him being homeless... that doesn't bother you?"

"He's not homeless now. He *was*. Past tense." I'm snippy, but I can't help it. I need Sabina to not pick apart this slice of happiness. "It's a communal house."

"Still... he eats food from a dumpster. That doesn't gross you out?"

I turn around to face her, my hand paused on a braid. "You sound like a snob."

"I'm not a snob. I—sometimes I worry about you with guys." She looks down at her lap.

"You *worry* about me? What are you talking about?"

"You get caught up with them easily. You slept with that Omar guy so quickly, and—don't you worry something's going to go wrong? He busks on the beach and lives with, like, a thousand people."

"You don't know him."

"Neither do *you*." She sighs, her eyes meeting mine again. "I'm not trying to be a jerk. I just wonder if this stuff is connected to your mom and maybe you need to talk to someone about it."

"Is Mama Jess training you to be a therapist or something? I don't have mommy issues." My hands are shaking. I can't believe she's saying this to me. Judging me. "And God, Sabina. You're acting like I fucked half a football team in one afternoon. Just because you want to wait to have sex until you get married doesn't mean I want to."

"I'm not saying you have mommy issues." She shakes her head. "I guess I don't know what I'm saying except I don't want you to get fucked over by this guy."

"Is it him, or is it anyone that I date?"

She frowns. "What?"

"Ever since I hooked up with Cody, you've been weird about me and guys. If it makes you uncomfortable, we don't have to talk about it, but I don't like you making me feel bad for doing what I want."

"I'm not jealous," she says firmly.

"I didn't say you were."

She runs a hand over the back of her head, fingers brushing absentmindedly down the woven strands of her French braids. "I think maybe I should go home."

"Yeah . . . maybe." It will take me twice as long to unbraid my hair alone, but I don't think Sabina and I can act like everything is normal after what we said to each other. We don't disagree often, and neither of us knows what to do about it.

I walk her to the door and we don't hug when we say good-bye, which is unprecedented. She waves at me stiffly and I stand at the door, watching her cross the lawn to her car parked by the curb.

Maybe I don't know Omar as well as I know Warren, but I know him better than she does. I know him well enough to understand that he makes me feel alive and good about who I am. He makes me feel less lonely, even when we're apart, and that feels like the best thing that's happened to me in a long time.

20.

It took two more tries—and one burned piecrust—but I finally got the lemon meringue to Lou's liking.

At first I thought his enthusiasm was forced, that he was just being nice to me because he felt bad that I'd had so much trouble with it. But as soon as I tried it myself, I was relieved that it tasted as good as it looked. My praise was earned.

I get to choose what I bake for him this time, and I wonder if that's a test, too. Like, maybe if I attempt something too difficult, he'll think I'm too arrogant to take seriously, but if I go too easy, he'll lose respect for me. I can't imagine how pressured my father felt, working right under him for so many years. Lou is the kind of guy you don't feel good about letting down.

After my braid appointment, I sit at the kitchen table with my mother's dessert cookbook, starting from page one. Looking at the table of contents, I wonder how many of these desserts are outdated and how many are considered classics. Warren is always saying that food goes through trends, too, and that no one will respect a chef who doesn't change with the times.

Lemon meringue seems like a mainstay, but what about a Baked Alaska? Although as soon as I see that it involves meringue, I can't turn the page fast enough. I flip through recipes for macarons (more meringue) and coconut macaroons, Boston cream pie and devil's food cake, bananas Foster and classic banana splits.

I've almost reached the end, wondering if I'll have to consult another cookbook, when I see exactly what I'm going to make: a French apple tart. The ingredients are simple enough, but the presentation is gorgeous, and if I can get it anywhere near the photo in this book, Lou will definitely be impressed.

I have to make a run to the grocery store, and it turns out post-dinnertime on a Saturday is a great time to shop for food because it's nearly empty when I get there. I took a picture of the ingredients list, but I have it memorized. I looked at the lemon meringue pie recipe so much it was practically imprinted on my eyeballs, and now it seems easier to just take a few extra minutes to absorb the list rather than having to look at it a million times while I'm working.

I'm in the produce aisle picking over a bin of Granny Smith apples when a memory hits me so hard it cuts through me like a knife.

The sweet, crisp smell of the fruit, the sight of it lined up neatly in rows, reminds me of standing next to an apple bin with my mother. She bought me an enormous caramel apple from the vendor and told me to wait right there, that she'd be back.

I was five, maybe six. She never should have left me alone anywhere, and especially not somewhere like the farmers' market, where someone could have snatched me up and disappeared in an instant. But she didn't go far.

She approached a guy standing next to one of the counters. I didn't know him, and I don't remember what he looked like. Tall? Back then, everyone was tall. All I remember is he wore a black baseball cap and he stood very close to her. The caramel on my apple was too sticky and tasted too sweet, so I watched them the whole time. I didn't understand that she would have taken me with her if whatever was going on was completely innocent, but I felt like something wasn't right.

My chest tightens so much that it's hard to take a breath. I can barely focus on the task of stuffing apples into a bag before I stumble my way through the checkout. Out at my car, I have to hold one of my hands steady with the other just to push the unlock button on my key fob. Once I'm in, I lean my forehead against the steering wheel and close my eyes.

Was that memory real? Is has to be—right? I couldn't just make up something like that after so many years. And if it's true, is the man in the baseball hat the reason she left us? The only person who'd have any idea is my father, and I can't ask him.

The last thing I feel like doing when I get home is making the tart, but Dad and I are taking it to Lou tomorrow, after my brunch with Warren and his father. I feel sluggish as I move about the kitchen, but at least the dough is already done. I made it last night after Sabina left. And that part was finally easy. I've worked with (and ruined) so much pastry dough by now that I feel like I could make it in my sleep.

The apples are an event. I have to peel each one and remove the middle with a melon baller, then slice them almost thin as paper. My hands shake every time I think of my mother at the farmers' market, and every once in a while I have to stop and set down the knife until they're steady once again.

I'm happy with the way the dough rolls out and the careful way I trim it and how I layer on the apples. Then I dot the top with cubes of butter, slide the tart into the oven, and wait.

It's times like this that I wish Omar could text because I don't feel like talking, just saying hi. I was worried things would feel weird between us after we slept together, but I didn't feel embarrassed or awkward. The most surprising part was probably how comfortable I was with him before, during, and after. I wish I could make Sabina understand.

Warren would get why this memory of my mom hit me so hard, but I can't bother him with that now. He's at work, and I know he's already sweating the meeting with his father tomorrow. I'm nervous enough *for* him.

The tart looks impeccable when I take it out of the oven an hour later: The edges of the pastry have appropriately browned, and the apple slices on top have a beautiful golden glow. The kitchen is warm and the air is sweet. The whole project has been easy from start to finish, but I don't feel good about it.

In fact, I can't get it out of my sight fast enough. I scribble FOR LOU on a piece of paper and drop it on top of the tart once it's cooled and covered. I don't want my father to forget and dig into it when he gets home.

I curl up on the couch in the living room and turn on the TV to a rerun marathon of an old sitcom. Just for noise. As my eyes start to close, I think I should move to my room, but I'm too comfortable here.

I wake to Dad shaking my shoulder, the remote in one hand. "You should go to bed, Yvonne. It's late."

I blink at him and rub my eyes. "What time is it?"

"Quarter to two."

"Oh." I blink again. "Dad?"

He's already heading toward the sunroom, his chef coat draped over his arm. He turns around. "Yeah?"

"Did Mom go to the farmers' market a lot?"

"Yvonne, what are you talking about?" He's been pretty patient with me until now, but this time he doesn't try to mask his irritation.

"I had this memory and I wanted to know if it's real. We were in a farmers' market, but I don't know where. And it was right before she left."

He sighs, and in the reflection from the television, I can see that his eyes are especially tired tonight. "Is there a reason you want to know all these things about your mother lately?"

I sit up halfway, balancing on one elbow. "We've never really talked about her. I don't *know* her. All I have to go on is what you can tell me. And you don't tell me much about anything."

"Yvonne..." He takes so long to respond that I wonder if he's going to answer me at all. He sighs again, through his nose this time. "I don't want you thinking just because Warren's father showed up, the same thing will happen to you. That's not how this stuff works."

"I'm not a child," I snap. "I know how it works. But it isn't fair that she left before I could really remember her. You had all this time with her...all these memories."

"It's not fair," he says quietly. "But there's nothing we can

180

do about it. I don't want you to get your hopes up for something that's never going to happen."

The finality of his statement stings. None of this is fair, and none of it is my fault. But I'm too tired to fight him on this. And I don't have to dig deep inside to know that what my father said is right.

21.

Warren barely looks at me when I get in his car before brunch the next morning.

"Hi." I wave a hand in front of his face when he doesn't say anything.

He finally glances over. "Hey. Hi. Sorry. I'm a little..."

"I know. Do you want me to drive?"

"No, I'll be all right." He offers a small smile. "You look great."

"Oh, thanks." I look down at my bright red tunic dress. I have a denim jacket with me, but it's still too hot to actually wear it here, even though it's late September. "The color isn't blinding you?"

"No more blinding than your beauty," he says with a straight face.

"Ew, shut up."

He ducks away from my good-natured swat, then quickly kisses under my ear. "Seriously, thanks for coming with me. I don't know if I'd be able to go through this alone."

Warren chose a new-ish restaurant downtown, a bright and airy spot with a long bar counter and modern decor. Outside the front door, he stops and turns to me.

"Do I look all right?" He's wearing dark jeans and a plain white T-shirt, and his hair looks freshly cut.

"You look like a son anyone would be happy to have. Ready?"

"Not really," he says. But he pushes through the front door and stands tall while he gives his name to the hostess, even as his fingers tremble by his side.

"The first guest has already arrived," she says with a sunny smile. "I'll show you to the table."

Warren inhales and looks at me before he follows the hostess. My eyes dart about, wondering if I'll be able to spot him before he sees us, but then we all stop and Warren is staring straight at his father.

"Your server will be right over," the hostess says, not at all registering the importance of what's happening here.

I get a good look at Warren's father when he stands. He's

about Warren's height, just under six feet, and their skin tones are almost identical. Perhaps the most similar thing about them is their eyes—his father's are a bright, bright blue, but they're the same shape with the same sleepy eyelids and long lashes. His hair is thinning but I can still make out some blond mixed in with the silver and white.

"Well, you certainly look like your picture," he says with a broad smile.

"They don't really bother to photoshop chefs." Warren's voice is dry as the desert.

His father's smile drops, just a little. "I sure appreciate you meeting me, Warren."

He nods.

"And who's this?"

Warren steps aside. "This is Yvonne."

"Hi." I stick out my hand, hoping to ease some of the discomfort. "Nice to meet you."

He looks relieved as we shake. "Nice meeting you, too."

There's an awkward moment where I don't know where I should sit, but Warren quickly takes the seat on the empty side of the table, leaving me to sit directly across from his father. Then there's an even more awkward moment when it appears that nobody is going to speak first.

I take one for the team. "Where do you live, Mr. . . . ?" I trail off, realizing I don't even know his name, first or last. Engel is Warren's mother's maiden name.

"Schroeder, but please call me Evan." His eyes shift to Warren as if to include him, too, as if he knows without a doubt that Warren won't be calling him dad. "I'm up from Orange County. We have a place down in Newport."

We. I don't have to look at Warren to see that he noticed, too. His shoulders stiffen.

"Warren, where do you live? Do you have roommates? I want to hear everything about you," Evan says, his voice warm.

Warren stares at him. "You first, *Evan.*"

Damn.

We pause to order drinks from the server. Evan looks a little conflicted as he glances over the menu, then finally orders a Bloody Mary. I think everyone at this table knows Warren isn't going to make this easy for him.

"I've been in Newport for about eighteen years. Had a brief stop in Huntington Beach." His eyes slide away from Warren when he says that part. He takes a long sip of coffee before he continues. "I'm married...with two kids."

I look down at my menu.

"What are their names?" Warren asks. He doesn't sound angry; in fact, there's no emotion at all behind his voice.

"They're twins. Oliver and Celeste." He pauses. "They just turned eleven."

Warren is silent.

"I understand that you're upset with me." Evan rests his

hands around the base of his coffee cup. "And I'll understand if you want to leave, now that you've seen me. But I promise I don't have any ill intent by contacting you, Warren. It's selfish, but I wanted to see the young man you've become. That article made me proud."

"The only person who gets to be proud of me is my mother," Warren says evenly. "You lost that right the second you left."

I'm starting to feel very much like I shouldn't be here, but I can't leave Warren. This is exactly why he needs me.

"And I was wrong to leave," Evan says, his eyes meeting Warren's.

He does look sincere, though I know Warren probably doesn't see what I do. I don't think I'd be at all rational if I were sitting across the table from my mother.

"I'm sorry, Warren," his father says. "I'm very, very sorry."

Warren's chair screeches as he pushes it back suddenly and bolts from the table. He goes back the way we came, all the way out the front door.

I look at Evan, whose lips are parted as he stares after him. "Should I go out there?"

"I'll go."

When I get outside, Warren is pacing by the side of the building. I say his name. He doesn't stop. I grip him by the shoulders, forcing him to stand still. When I look up, his eyes are red and his lashes are wet.

"Oh, Warren."

He lets out a shaky breath. "I can't decide if I hate him more because of what he did or because he seems like a normal dude who just made a mistake."

"You can feel however you feel," I say, lightly rubbing his back. I've never seen him cry before.

"I *feel* like an asshole for running out of there."

"If anyone should understand, it's the man who ran out on *you* when you were a baby." I pause. "He was going to come out here, but I told him I would."

"Really?"

"Yeah. War, I don't want to tell you what to think, but maybe you should see if it's worth giving him a chance. He—"

"I love you."

I stare at him. "Why are you saying this now?"

"Because I can't keep it inside anymore. And you're here with me . . . and this is one of the hardest things I've ever had to go through. And . . . I love you."

I'm not surprised, but this is the first time he's actually said it. He's said that he's *falling* for me, that he *cares* about me, but never *love*. I like the sound of those words. They feel right, from Warren's lips to my ears. And I feel warm all over. Until I think of Omar and how it would crush Warren if he knew about him.

"Warren . . ."

"Sorry. I know this isn't the time or the place, but I do."

His eyes are shining as he looks down at me. I don't recognize his expression. No one has looked at me like this before, but I know that it makes me happy. I know that what he's saying is true.

I hug him, for a long time. I don't know what to say, and it's the best way to express how much I appreciate him.

"Should we go back inside?" I finally ask.

He doesn't seem upset that I didn't verbally return the sentiment. He looks content, like he's said what he needed to say. Like he's ready to go back in and face Evan—minus all the fire and brimstone.

"I guess so. I feel silly for being all dramatic."

"Are you kidding? Some actors would kill for a performance like that."

He grins and then he takes my hand and we walk back inside together.

After brunch, Warren asks me to come back to his apartment; he doesn't want to be alone. He's buzzing with nervous energy. Dad and I aren't going to Lou's until dinnertime, so I say yes.

His place is the messiest I've ever seen it, which is to say it still isn't all that messy. But a bunch of clothes are piled on the bed and the floor around his closet, and it makes me smile, thinking of Warren trying to find the best outfit to meet Evan.

"Want something to eat?" he asks, wandering idly to the kitchen.

"We just ate." Though he barely touched his pancakes and instead chugged coffee the whole time.

"Right. God!" He shakes his head. "I still can't believe I met him."

"What did you think? I mean, after we went back in." Warren was pretty silent on the drive back. He looked so dazed that I kept glancing over to make sure he was paying attention to the road.

"He's an asshole for what he did to me and my mom. I don't know if I can forgive him for that, but I don't think he's a terrible guy."

"Do you think you'll stay in touch?"

Warren shrugs. "I don't know. That might be going a little far."

"No one's going to judge you for wanting to get to know him."

He pulls a beer from the fridge, even though it's barely past noon, and joins me on the futon. "Not even my mom?" He cracks it open, takes a swig, and passes it to me.

I take a sip. It's strange to be drinking beer when it's sunny out—the same way I feel when eating breakfast for dinner. "I think even she would get it. He's your family."

"No, he's my blood. There's a difference."

I don't disagree, but I've always thought of my mother as

family. Maybe because she was around longer than Warren's father was. Or maybe because my dad is so removed from my life, I'm desperate to claim what I can.

"You know what made me feel better, though?" He pauses, like he's trying to think of the best way to articulate his thoughts. "When he showed me that picture of his family."

"I couldn't believe you asked to see it! I thought you wanted to kill him when he told you he had twins."

"Yeah, I kind of did. But I had to know what they looked like...and I was really fucking relieved to see that they're black. I thought maybe it would piss me off if they were, like maybe he was one of those white dudes with a fetish for black women. And maybe he is—I don't know him." Warren sighs. "But I want to believe he's not a total piece of shit, you know? I want to believe he really loved my mom.... That he didn't leave her just because he couldn't handle having a black wife *and* a black kid."

"I get it," I say. I've never thought of whom my mother would have run off with—if she'd run off with anybody at all. I wish I remembered more about the guy in the baseball cap all those years ago.

We pass the beer back and forth until it's gone, then Warren says he's exhausted and wants to take a nap. I join him.

Omar and I didn't get much of a chance to laze about after we slept together. He had to catch his train in time to make it back to Venice, and he also had to make sure he was out of there before my dad got home. I wonder, if we'd held each other, if it would have felt like it does with Warren. I fit neatly into the space under his arm, and I love draping my arm over his chest, feeling the rise and fall of it beneath my skin.

I guess he wasn't the only one who was exhausted because we wake up two hours later. I stretch long and lean like a cat. Warren groans himself awake, rubbing at his eyes. He turns to face me. I'm still staring up at the ceiling when I feel his palm slide over my stomach.

"Hey," he says.

I look over and he kisses me. There may be a time when I don't want Warren, but that time is not now.

Maybe it's all the emotion from brunch, or perhaps it's the fact that he told me he loves me, but I am hungry for him. Our kisses are slow and tender; they linger. Warren's hands are everywhere—slipping down my calves and under my dress, sliding up my thighs and between my legs. I gasp and bite my lip when he touches me.

He pulls off my dress and underwear and unhooks my bra, and as his hands roam over me, he murmurs about how soft my skin is. Like silk, I think he says, but I'm not really listening because his hands are magic.

I've just slid his shirt over his shoulders and am kissing my way down his chest when he says, "I want you, Yvonne."

"I want you, too." I slide my lips over his ribs.

"No, I mean, I *want* you."

I look at him. "I know. Me too."

His jeans and boxers are off in seconds, and then we're just sitting there looking at each other, completely nude and finally here.

"I got tested," he says. "Just a few weeks ago, before your birthday. I'm clean."

"I trust you, but . . . you have condoms?"

"Of course. I just wanted you to know."

He pulls a condom from his nightstand. When he turns around, I put my hands on either side of his face and kiss him. "We're really doing this."

"Yeah," he says, not able to hide the big smile that takes over his face. "We're really doing this."

Moments later, Warren is inside me, and it's our first time but it feels like our bodies were meant for each other. It feels like no one else will ever know how to touch me the way he does. Every part of this feels right.

"War?"

He stops moving. "You okay?"

"Yeah, I just—I wanted to say I love you, too."

He smiles. Kisses a straight line over the contours of my face: my forehead, my nose, and my lips.

"I love you so much, Yvonne," he breathes.

PART 2.

22.

'm late.

Fuck.

PART 3.

23.

Sabina and I haven't been the same since the night she left my house upset.

We took a couple of days afterward to ourselves, and it was so unsettling not to hear from her for two whole days that I almost caved and texted. So many times. I almost said I was sorry, even though I didn't think I had anything to be sorry about. She must have felt the same way because we didn't talk until the following Monday, when we saw each other at school.

The tension between us has lessened, but we never did discuss that evening. We eat lunch together and text dozens of times a day, but it's been a little over three weeks and we are still strained.

She looks surprised when I'm waiting by her locker after school. It pains me, the wedge that's grown between us. It's not large, but it's not like us. I hate it.

"I need you to go somewhere with me," I say.

She opens her locker and transfers some books from her bag to the shelf. "What's wrong?"

"We just have to go somewhere. Now. It's...sort of an emergency."

She pauses, looking at me. "Are you okay?"

"I'm late," I whisper.

She blinks at me with wide eyes as the meaning sinks in. "Oh my God. Omar?" She whispers his name.

I swallow. "Or Warren."

"*What?*"

"I didn't tell you because things get weird with us when we talk about that stuff. I didn't want to make it any weirder."

"Yvonne." She shakes her head. "Yeah, things have been weird, but this is—have you taken a test?"

I look around the hall to see if anyone is listening, but no one is paying attention. "Not yet."

She zips her bag and closes her locker. "Come on. We're going to the drugstore."

"You don't have anything to do?"

"It wouldn't matter if I did. Like you said, it's an emergency."

Sabina not only drives me to the store, but she goes in and buys the test while I wait in the car.

"Three different kinds," she says when I'm staring into the bag, confused by all the boxes. "That way you won't have to wonder if it's a bad test or a bad brand or whatever."

"You sound like you've done this before." The joke comes out easily but there's no humor in my voice.

She smiles anyway. "I'm channeling my inner Mom. She takes everything seriously. Your house or mine? My parents won't be home for a while, so it's safe."

"Mine." My dad won't be home until late, and I don't want to take any chances of seeing her moms.

Sabina has already done a lot for me today, but if she could take the test for me, I'd let her.

"I'll be right here," she says, standing in the hallway as I close the door.

The first test I choose takes only a minute to give results. I pee on the stick and burst out of the room, leaving it on the counter.

"You already know?"

"No, I just can't be in there with it. Alone. Will you look for me?"

She goes in. I count to sixty in my head. There's no sound from the bathroom. Which can't be good.

"Sabs?"

She walks back out, her mouth open. "It's positive."

I feel like someone has knocked the breath out of me, but there's still a chance it could be wrong. I down two glasses of water before I take the next two, wanting to hold on to that little bit of hope—that just maybe this will go my way in the end. Lots of girls have pregnancy scares. Why should this be any different for me? Tests aren't 100 percent accurate.

And condoms aren't 100 percent safe.

I set down my glass, go back into the bathroom, and take the next two tests. My hands shake as I try to hold the sticks steady because what if the first one wasn't wrong?

It wasn't. The other two are positive.

I slide down the wall until I'm sitting on the hallway floor, my forehead pressed to my knees. I feel like I'm outside of myself, watching from a distance, but I also feel like I knew the whole time. As soon as I realized I was late, I knew. Is that possible?

Sabina drops to her knees, rubbing my back. "It's going to be okay."

"I'm *pregnant*, Sabina." My voice is muffled, but she hears me loud and clear.

"I just mean...no matter what you decide, I'm here for you."

"My dad is going to be so pissed at me."

"Yvonne, it happens." She pauses. "And you don't have to tell him if you don't want to."

"It's not supposed to happen to *me*. He doesn't care what

I do most of the time, but getting pregnant..." I shake my head. Take a deep breath before I go on. "I know I don't have to tell him, but I feel cheated, not having my mom here. I hate feeling like I don't have anyone I can go to with this kind of stuff, just because he's my dad. Just because he can't handle anything personal."

Sabina is still rubbing my back, her hand making small, comforting circles through my shirt.

I release a shaky breath. "He barely talks to me now. I don't want him to pull away even more. I don't want him to be ashamed of me."

"He's your dad. He'll love you no matter what."

I nod but I don't lift my head. I don't say anything, and I don't move from the hallway. Neither does Sabina. She sits with me for the rest of the afternoon and then, when it's time for dinner, she calls Mama Jess and tells her she won't be home.

Sabina persuades me to move to my bed, and she orders in food that I don't eat. She doesn't try to get me to talk, and she takes away the food when I refuse it.

I ache for some sort of release. Hysterical tears, shouting, incoherent rambling—anything to make me feel present. Alive.

But I feel nothing.

When it gets late, Sabina sets a glass of water on my

nightstand. Then she turns out the light and climbs into bed and holds me.

Loneliness leaves me feeling a lot of things: sad, angry, betrayed. Sometimes I think I could choke on it. But I prefer it to numbness.

Numbness is nothing, and that feels unfixable.

24.

Omar is missing.

We haven't seen each other since we had sex, and we've only talked once. Part of that is because I was still processing what happened with Warren. As soon as I told him I loved him, I knew I couldn't be with Omar again. Not without feeling an immense amount of guilt about and betrayal to Warren.

But that doesn't mean I'm not annoyed I haven't heard from Omar. He doesn't seem like the type of guy who would just disappear. He's always shown up when we have plans—been exactly where he's said he'll be, and usually early. He never left me alone when I went to his house, except for when he was playing—and even then, he made sure I was only a few feet away. This seems out of character, and I'm starting to wonder if something has happened.

Even before I got pregnant, I wondered what people would think if they knew I'd been with Omar and Warren not even a week apart. I can't imagine they'd have anything nice to say, though we were careful. Even though I liked both of them and wanted it just as much as they did. Even though I wasn't in a committed relationship with either of them and did nothing wrong.

Maybe there would have been potential for more with Omar if Warren hadn't been around. I am attracted to him—his looks, his personality, his musical talent. The timing isn't right for us, even though I like spending time with him. I like how he makes me feel—open and free. Enraptured. We aren't together, so there will be no breakup, but I need closure. Especially before I talk to Warren.

I don't know if I'll tell Omar about the pregnancy. It's too soon to know what I want to do. Every time I think about that day with Sabina, I wonder if I imagined the positive tests lined up on the bathroom counter. At least four times a day, I fool myself into believing it's all a dream and I'll wake up not pregnant.

I call Omar again and again, but he never picks up. There is no voicemail, and of course I can't text him. I keep calling and calling until I become so tired of getting no answer, I decide to track him down.

I start close to home. He works a couple of days a week at the Cooper Youth Center, which is just downtown, so I go there first, rather than drive all the way to Venice. I don't know why I didn't think of this sooner. I don't know why we haven't seen each other more when he's over on my side of town twice a week. Maybe he's embarrassed about his lack of money and the fact that he has no car, but I thought I made it clear that those things don't matter to me.

I've never been to the youth center. It's easy to find, located in a nondescript building next to a parking garage. Inside, it smells like a cross between a locker room and a cafeteria, and the walls are painted with murals of kids of multiple races and ethnicities surrounded by books and soccer balls and baseball bats and animals and splashes of big golden suns.

A young woman with golden-brown skin and long, silky black hair is sitting at the front desk. She looks up and smiles. "Hi, how can I help you?"

I wait until I'm standing right in front of her until I speak. I don't want Omar to overhear me if he's nearby. I'm already embarrassed to be here, but I don't know how else to get a hold of him.

"I'm looking for Omar?"

It occurs to me then that I don't know his last name. I thought about asking him a couple of times, but then I'd get distracted and forget, and I guess it just never seemed all that important.

Her eyebrows knit together. "Omar?"

"Yeah, he said he works on Tuesdays and Thursdays." She might be new, so I add, "He teaches violin."

"Oh, I thought you meant one of the kids. No, we don't have anyone with that name who works here."

My stomach sinks. "Are you sure? Black guy with dreads?"

She shakes her head. "Our staff is small, and I'm in charge of payroll. There's no one here by that name. We actually don't have anyone who teaches strings right now."

"Okay." I want to tell her to think harder or ask if she'll let me go in back to look for him, but I know I wouldn't find him. "Thanks for your help."

"No problem." She pauses, then: "I hope you find your friend."

"Yeah, me too. Thanks."

Why would he lie to me about working here? I don't know him that well, but he doesn't seem like a liar. Every word he's spoken has seemed so sincere. I never once got the feeling I couldn't trust him. The little details of his family and his past don't matter so much as how we feel when we're around each other. And now I wonder how much of that was a lie, too.

I get back in my car and drive to the beach because I don't know where else to look for him. I check his normal spot, but neither he nor Keely are there. No chairs, no violin, no Omar. The sick feeling in my stomach spreads.

I walk up and down the whole boardwalk, scanning all the booths. I poke my head into the burger place we went to and peer through the windows of the other bars and restaurants. I look out over the skate park and scour Muscle Beach. He's not here.

There's one more place to look. I've only been there once, but I remember the way to the communal house. And it doesn't look any better in the fading daylight.

I walk up the front steps. Through the screen door, I see a couple of guys in the front room, rolling a joint.

"Hi," I call out.

One of them looks over. "Hey, what's up?"

"Is Omar here?"

"Nope. He and Keely won't be back till next week."

"Next week? Where'd they go?"

He spins a lighter on the coffee table. "On tour or something? Keely got a gig, and he went with her."

"Oh."

He must hear the disappointment in my voice because he says, "Wanna smoke up with us?"

"No, I'm good. Next week, you said?"

"Yeah, next Wednesday, 'cause they've got someone subletting their room while they're gone, and they gotta be out by then."

I thank him and trudge down the steps and back to my car. I have an answer now, but I don't feel any better. Why did Omar even bring up the youth center that day? It's gross, pretending to work with kids who would need him the most. And I can't shake the nagging feeling that there's still something there with Keely. Why else would he go on tour with her? The guy said *Keely* got the gig, not both of them.

The worst part is I have no one to talk to about this. I can't tell Warren, of course. Sabina has been great, checking on me all the time, but I don't want to give her another reason to judge me. I didn't regret sleeping with Omar, but now I am so embarrassed. I feel stupid for believing his lie, no matter how small.

At home, my violin is still sitting by the front door where I put it down after school. I glare at it. I never would have gotten caught up with Omar if it wasn't for that thing. I open the case with visions of smashing it to splinters on the foyer tile, of snapping the bow in half over my knee. That would make the choice for me about my future.

But instead, I pull it out of the case and slip it under my chin. I play everything I can think of. First, the Vivaldi from the night I was with Omar because I was so angry when I played it last time, it seems like a good outlet now. I move on to the Prokofiev piece we heard that night, the "Montagues and Capulets," because I've always felt so good about it. I need it. There's nothing that makes me feel more powerless than being lied to, and this is the antidote.

My arms are tired, and still I move on to the Haydn

concerto we're working on in class. I should be better, but I remember enough for it to be recognizable, and that's good enough for now. I play and I play until I start to get sloppy and the notes muddle together and my neck starts to hurt. I am sweating when I put down my violin, and I'm shocked to see an hour has passed.

I feel better than I have in weeks, maybe months. Not because it was perfect—far from it. I needed to feel better, to express my emotions through my music, and it worked. I wasn't playing for Ortiz or Denis or Omar. I wasn't playing to impress anyone or prove that I'm good enough to attend a conservatory or perform in a symphony.

I was playing for me.

25.

Knowing there's something growing inside me doesn't make me feel less alone.

But I don't really want to be with other people. Sabina has been wonderful, even with the weirdness still hovering over us. It's sort of like we put our disagreement on hold because we had to—because of my situation. She checks on me all the time at school and at home: to see how I'm feeling, if I need anything to eat or drink, if I want to talk about anything. She offers to drive me anywhere I want to go, but there's nowhere I want to be.

It's only been a week since I found out, but I don't feel that different. Not yet. No morning sickness. I'm not showing. And even though I know it's way too early, I check for changes every morning and night in the full-length mirror, examining myself from as many angles as possible.

I did ask Sabina to drive me to Planned Parenthood the day after I went looking for Omar, so I could get another test. My fourth. The nurse, who was kind and patient with me even as I asked a never-ending list of questions, said I could get a blood test if I wanted to but that the urine tests are quite accurate. And for the fourth time, I learned that I am pregnant.

I got tested for STDs, too, after Sabina suggested it. I hated that she was right; it made me feel even more foolish about Omar. Because the truth is, I was so caught up in the moment with him that I forgot to ask about the last time he was tested…and now I'm not so sure he would have been honest with me, anyway.

Sabina held my hand. The nurse's voice was filled with empathy as she discussed my options, all of which I already knew: I can see the pregnancy to full term and have a child that I keep, I can see the pregnancy to full term and give up the child for adoption, or I can have an abortion. I declined the brochures. It was the oddest feeling, listening to someone confirm the biggest problem I've ever had to face while alternately feeling like I was in the safest, most supportive space ever.

I've been spending a lot of time in the sunroom when my father isn't home. I eat snacks and meals and do homework in there, even though it takes me forever because I can't seem to focus on anything. I have to reread whole pages and double-check all my work. And it feels like I'm already doing twice the work because I'm barely present in class; there in body only.

Today I go into the room immediately after school and lie down on the chaise. I've felt more tired than normal in the past week, but I don't know if that's because of the pregnancy or because I know it's an early symptom. Maybe it's just the exhaustion from constantly thinking about what I'm going to do.

I've never really thought about what I'd choose if I got pregnant. I guess I never thought I'd *get* pregnant before I wanted to, despite my father's warning. I guess I should have been on birth control. I guess one of the condoms broke. I felt safe and supported at Planned Parenthood, but I was still embarrassed. Hopeful that the nurse believed me when I said I'd used protection both times. I get the feeling she would have been just as empathetic if I hadn't.

I've never had a mothering instinct. Some girls at Courtland have been talking about their ten-year plans, how they'll go to undergrad, then grad school, then immediately get married and start having children. That sounds so boring to me, planning out my life like that. I still don't know what I want to do and when, but I think I want to travel. I want to meet more people and see new places and eat food that even my father hasn't tried. A lot of that seems harder to do if I had a baby. Even college sounds daunting. People do it, but I can't imagine raising a child while trying to hold down a serious load of classes. Or working full-time. Those people seem like superheroes to me.

But then I think of what it would actually be like to have a family of my own. What would it feel like to be needed and wanted by someone instead of just happening to live with a person who is related to me? I think of Warren and how well we fit together. I wonder if we could ever be parents together. I wonder what he will do when I tell him—because I am going to tell him. No matter what I decide, I want Warren to know.

I close my eyes and try to think of anything except the pregnancy...but then my mother comes to mind. I wonder if she wanted me as soon as she found out she was pregnant or if she struggled over her decision. It's hard to imagine she'd always wanted a child; she left so soon after entering into the deal. What if she'd wanted an abortion and didn't get it? What if she wanted me at first and then changed her mind?

It's always been buried deep in the internal collection of things I don't want to think about, the possibility that I drove my mother away. But now I wonder if that's why my father has been so vague about her all these years. That's not something you can admit to your child.

As much as I hoped I could find the answers in the walls of this room, being in here doesn't help. I don't feel the presence of my mother, and I don't have any idea what she would have done if she were in my place. I don't feel anything at all in here, and that's the worst part.

I peel myself off the chaise to go to the kitchen. I owe Lou another French apple tart. He couldn't articulate what was wrong with the first one. He simply said something was off. I don't mind making another one. In fact, I can't think of a better way to keep myself busy.

I take the tart up to Mount Washington the next evening.

Lou told me to come over for dinner because he's making a whole roasted chicken that will take him days to eat by himself.

He opens the door wearing his usual gray T-shirt and big smile. "Apple tart, take two?"

"Just for you." I hold out the covered pie plate in my hands.

The smell of roasting chicken permeates the air, and for the first time since I realized my period was late, I feel hungry. Like I'm actually looking forward to eating. Everything has tasted like paper.

During dinner, Lou mentions Claudia—how she was the one who taught him the best way to roast a chicken so that it came out tender and juicy with golden, crispy skin.

"She never wanted to take credit for it," he says, looking

wistfully out the large bay window of the dining room, "but she was the inspiration for many of my dishes. She always knew how to make food better, even when I thought it was already perfect."

"Lou?"

He glances over sharply, as if I've jarred him back into the present. As if he were seeing Claudia in the distant mountaintops.

"Why did you and Claudia never have kids?"

"Well, I guess it was one of those things where we always thought we had time. We knew we didn't want to be young parents. We wanted to see the world and visit every restaurant with a Michelin star and make sure we didn't miss out on our own lives." He takes a sip of water. "And then it never seemed like a good idea to have a kid when I'd just opened a restaurant, so we held off...and then it was too late."

I spear a garlicky brussels sprout with the end of my fork. "Do you regret it?"

"Not at the time. We were so busy, and life moves so fast." He pauses. "But after she died? Yes. I wish we'd had children. I'd give anything to have someone here who was a part of her...someone we'd made together."

Under the table, my hands instinctively go to my stomach.

"I'm sorry, Lou."

He smiles. "Oh, it's not as sad as all that. I had many years with Claud, and she was my true love. Some people will never be that lucky."

I want to leave the table when he brings out the tart, but I know I have to sit here and listen to whatever he has to say. It's part of the deal.

This one is just as pretty as the last, but I felt different while I was making it. A part of my brain shut off when I began crafting the dough—a part that allowed me to take pure pleasure in the act of baking. I didn't think about the fact that I am pregnant or how Lou would judge my second attempt at the tart; my brain didn't even flicker on the image of my mother at the farmers' market, talking to the strange man. Creating this tart was like a balm for my soul.

"This is it!" Lou exclaims after swallowing his first bite. He's grinning so proudly, you'd think I'd just won a televised baking competition. "*This* is what I'm looking for. Technical proficiency, excellent taste, exquisite presentation."

My cheeks are hot from his praise. "Really?"

I take a bite and that answers my question. The crust is perfectly flaky; the apple slices beautifully caramelized, and the apricot jam brushed across the top is just the right complement to the tartness of the Granny Smiths. I knew this version felt different, but I wasn't sure if I'd actually achieved what I thought I did. It took me so long to realize how my relationship with violin had changed, I'm never quite certain if I can trust in my abilities.

"It's fantastic, Yvonne. What did you do differently this time?"

218

"Nothing," I say slowly. "But I guess...it seemed like I was in a different state of mind, if that makes sense."

He forks up another bite and nods thoughtfully. "Yes, of course it does. Sinclair isn't very flowery, so he probably never talks about this, but I wholeheartedly believe that the amount of love you put into your food reflects back in the finished product. How were you feeling when you made the first tart?"

"It was the last thing I wanted to do."

"What was different this time?"

I'm pregnant. But I can't say that.

I'm not sure I can articulate what was different, just that I let everything go and concentrated fully on the preparation. As if the French apple tart would be the most important task of my life. And it felt right, like the other night when I played the violin at home for the first time in a long time. I was doing what I was supposed to be doing—not only for Lou, but for myself.

"I don't know. Maybe I'm learning."

He leans against the counter. "Are you enjoying this setup we have?"

"Yeah...I am." I press the tip of my index finger into the crumbs on my plate. "I never expected to, but it's kind of nice."

"Just kind of?"

I frown at him. "What are you saying?"

"Well," he begins, looking at the tart before moving his gaze to me. "If you really like baking and you want to learn even more, I'd love it if you staged at my restaurant for a while."

"Stage?" He pronounces it with an *ah* sound, and it's a term I'm not familiar with.

"It's our word for internships in restaurant kitchens. Staging was what chefs did before the culinary school boom, but it's still prevalent today. I did it and your father did it. Warren staged at my restaurant before he went to work for your father. It's a good way to see the inner workings of a kitchen and test yourself."

"You'd do that for me?" But when I think about it too much, I wonder if it was Lou's idea at all. Has he been conspiring with my father this whole time? Dad likes it when I have something to keep me busy. Maybe this was his way of trying to help since I told him I wouldn't be applying to music programs.

"I—I don't know what to say," I begin, then stop. "That's so nice, Lou, but I'm not good enough to be a pastry chef."

"You are," he says easily.

"But I've never worked in a kitchen before." I'm trying to force him into saying this isn't worth my time because I can't believe he thinks I have natural talent. Just because you enjoy something doesn't mean you're good enough to pursue it. I'm too old to dupe myself into believing that again.

"Which is precisely why you'd be staging. To learn. I wouldn't suggest you go for this if I didn't believe you could excel. And then if things go well, perhaps we'd look at enrolling you in a proper pastry chef program. You know, there's a very famous one in Paris that I've always wondered about...."

Staging. Culinary school. Paris. My brain is spinning. I'm finding it hard to come up with words. Where will I be in a year? Or six months? I don't know what choice I'm going to make in the next few *weeks*. These potential plans are exciting, but I wonder if they'll still be an option for me, whatever I decide to do about my current problem.

"Your father and I didn't jump to where we are overnight," Lou says. "Even the most talented people have to work hard to become the best. Writers don't just pop out award-winning novels on their first try. We all have different paths, and we all learned a lot along the way. From school, our peers, our mentors."

"Have you talked to my dad about this? You're..." It's hard for me to say the words, but I have to know. "You're not just doing this for me because you like him?"

Lou shakes his head firmly. "I don't have time to waste on someone who doesn't have potential. And maybe I'm wrong, but you and I seem to have our own relationship independent of your dad. As your godfather, I'm pretty proud of that."

I smile at him shyly, glad that he likes our time together as much as I do. "You're not wrong."

"Good. And I haven't told your father what I just proposed, but he won't be surprised. I used to give him little tests like these when he was starting out. He was furious with me during the beef bourguignonne assignment—I made him go back to the kitchen ten times before it was good enough."

That makes me laugh. Patience isn't one of my dad's strongest qualities, which doesn't pair well with his lifelong quest for perfection.

"Just promise me you'll think about it," Lou says, cutting another piece of the tart.

"I promise."

26.

Warren has a rare Saturday off, so when I tell him earlier in the week that we need to talk, he says to come over that night.

I wish I could blurt out my news over the phone because I don't want to see Warren's face when I tell him. I usually know what to expect with him, but this is the most serious thing I've ever had to talk to him about, by far. And every time I think about how I have to explain Omar, I want to cancel on him and stay home.

I don't feel any better when I get to his place. I planned to stand outside the door for a few moments to calm my nerves before I went in, but Warren must have heard my footsteps on the stairs because he pops his head out before I've stepped onto the doormat.

He pulls me into the apartment and kisses me. He smells so good, like he's just showered. His hair is still damp.

"That was a nice greeting," I say when our lips part.

"I guess I missed you," he says. "It's been a few days. . . . I was starting to think you were avoiding me."

I shake my head. Then, when he kisses me again, his hand slides lightly across my stomach and I jump back immediately, startling both of us.

"What's wrong?"

"Nothing, I . . ." I trail off because when I look over his shoulder, I notice the table in the background.

It's set for two, and he's done it up with a crisp white tablecloth and folded cloth napkins. Two long white candlesticks sit in the center, tips freshly lit and glowing.

I look around. I was so caught off guard when I came in that I didn't realize the entire room is bathed in candlelight.

"This is me trying to make up for your birthday." He lifts my hand to his lips and kisses the back of it. "Better late than never, right?"

"You didn't have to do this, War," I say softly.

"I wanted to." He smiles. "I even got another cake."

And then, after I've seen all the trouble he went to, making me dinner on his night off, I know I can't tell him until later tonight. After we've eaten. It doesn't seem right to let all this food and his efforts go to waste. My appetite is already shaky; I won't be able to eat a bite after we talk.

"I got some wine," he says. "Red and white. And I have beer, too. I sprang for the good stuff."

"Um, actually, I'm good with water."

Warren frowns. "You hungover from last night?"

"No, I didn't go out. I just don't feel like drinking," I say, hoping my voice is strong enough to be believable.

Even if I end up having an abortion, drinking doesn't seem like the greatest idea in my current emotional state. I burst into tears this morning while watching a milk commercial.

Warren starts us off with a cheese plate on which he's artfully arranged some Brie, Gouda, and manchego, along with a handful of almonds, crusty bread, and a small jar of cherry preserves. I nibble at a little bit of everything except the Brie—I hate Brie and he loves it, something we've argued about far too often—while he talks about the new cheese shop he visited in Eagle Rock.

"They recognized me from the *SoCal Weekly* piece," he says, pride shining through in his voice.

"Do you feel better about the article now?"

He smears a glob of preserves onto a hunk of bread. "I think I felt better about it after seeing my dad."

"Have you talked to him since the brunch?"

"We've been emailing some, but I'm keeping my distance.

I'm not ready to have dinner with him and his family or whatever." He sighs. "I haven't told my mom yet."

"Are you going to?" I've met his mom a few times. She's a sweet but no-nonsense woman with Warren's smile.

"If I see him again, yeah. . . . Does this make you want to find your mom?"

"Yes and no. I feel like if she wanted to be found, I'd have already found her, you know?" And my father made it very clear that this probably won't happen, no matter how much I've wished for it.

"It's her loss, then," he says. "Completely."

Warren serves rack of lamb next. He leans over my shoulder to place the platter on the table, then dips his head to kiss my earlobe before he returns to his seat. The lamb is cooked to a beautiful medium rare, just the way we both like it, and the outside of the chops are crusted with fresh herbs. I can smell the rosemary and thyme before I begin cutting into the meat.

This is by far the most romantic dinner I've ever sat down to, and I can't fully enjoy it since I have no idea where things will stand with us after I tell him.

"So, you wanted to talk?" he says as if he's peeked into my thoughts. But his voice is so light he couldn't have guessed what it is.

"It can wait."

"Well, good, because I wanted to talk to you, too." He clears his throat. "I know things were a little rocky with us for a while, but I love you, Yvonne, and I don't want to see anyone else."

I pause in cutting my lamb chop. "You want to be exclusive?"

"Yeah," he says almost shyly, and then his face pinkens. "I want you to be my girlfriend."

I take exactly one bite of lamb before I start to cry.

"Whoa, whoa, whoa." He stares at me, confused. "I thought everything was good with us or I wouldn't have—"

"Everything's great with us, Warren," I choke out. "But not with me."

He shakes his head, not understanding.

My voice is so wobbly I don't know if he'll comprehend what I'm saying. But if I wait to speak until it's steady and strong, we'll be waiting forever.

"What did you say?" He leans forward as if the extra few inches will make a difference. The table is tiny. Our knees touch underneath.

My voice hiccups on every word the next time I try. He still doesn't understand.

I close my eyes the third time. It's a lot easier to say something so difficult when I don't have to look at him. "I'm pregnant."

There is no sound. Not a peep. It's so quiet that the dull hum of the refrigerator is loud as a bullhorn.

When I open my eyes, Warren is staring at my plate, his

mouth slack. The color has drained from his face. He breathes in and out a couple of times, but he doesn't move. Just stares.

"Warren?"

He blinks and swallows. "I—wow. This is—this isn't what I expected. I mean, we were safe, right? Every time?"

We've only been together a few times since that first afternoon, and we used a condom each time. I insisted on it.

"Yes, but Warren . . . there's more."

"Oh, God. Have you told Sinclair?" He looks more upset about the prospect of my father knowing than me being pregnant, which makes me feel as if the blood in my veins has been replaced by hot lava.

"Jesus, Warren! Not *everything* is about my fucking father!" I practically shout.

"Okay, sorry. You're right." He picks up the napkin from his lap, squeezing it into a ball with one hand. "Go on."

I close my eyes again, but it doesn't help this time. The words are still stuck in my throat, and after a while, I feel stupid sitting here with my eyes closed, in complete silence. I can't look at him, though, so I focus on my lamb. The pink-ness of it, which looked so appealing a few minutes ago, turns my stomach.

"I was seeing someone," I say in a low voice. "It wasn't serious, but I was with him . . . the week before our first time. Only once, but—"

"But you slept with him."

"Yes." My eyes burn a hole into my plate.

"The week before our first time together."

"Yes," I whisper.

Warren's chair screeches back so quickly that it topples over. He doesn't right it. He walks to the kitchen, like he's going to serve our next course, but he only stays there for a second before he's stalking across the floor to the other side of the room.

"So you don't know whose it is?" His voice is wooden.

"No, Warren. I don't." My heart is in my throat.

"Did you use protection?"

"Does it *matter* at this point?"

"*Yes*, Yvonne, it goddamn matters! You hooked up with some random guy and then you slept with me. I deserve to know if I could have some sort of disease. What if our condom broke and—"

"Fuck you, Warren. Of course I used protection. You think I would do that to you?"

"I honestly don't know what you're capable of."

I jump up from the table and throw my napkin to the floor. That isn't satisfying enough, so I sweep the silverware off the table, too. Then I march over to him until we're standing face-to-face.

"You don't get to talk to me like I'm garbage just because I was with someone else. You and I weren't exclusive. You abandoned me on my birthday to score points with my dad, even though you knew how much it would hurt me. You *know* how hard that day is for me, and you still fucked it up. So don't you dare talk to me about *possibly* hurting you when you *actually* hurt me and I'm still here."

He doesn't say anything and he doesn't look at me, but I can see he's breathing rapidly. When he speaks again, his voice is low. Restrained.

"I'm sorry. I'm just... This is a shock. Do you know what you're going to do?"

I shake my head. "The woman at Planned Parenthood said I can check paternity a few ways, but you have to wait until you're a certain number of weeks, and I don't think I can do that."

I can't sit around letting this... *thing* grow inside me, waiting to learn whose it is. What if I don't like the result? What if I decide by the time I find out that I don't want it, no matter who the father is?

"So you're going to have an abortion." His tone isn't judgmental, and it's not that wooden voice from before. It's somewhere in between, and that doesn't make me feel any better.

"I'm not sure." I hesitate before what I say next, because there's a very good chance he's not going to give me an answer I like. But I have to know. "If it was yours... would you want me to keep it?"

He swallows hard, his Adam's apple bobbing. "I don't know."

230

He doesn't look at me, and somehow that seems more hurtful than his words. I don't know what I want, either, but this feels like rejection. It feels fucking terrible.

"I'm going to go." I walk to the futon, where I dropped my bag earlier.

"Yvonne..."

I can't stick around here. I don't blame him for not having the answers, for not saying exactly what I wanted to hear, because I'm not sure what that would be.

But I can't stay in this room and listen to him work out his feelings on this.

I can't make him feel okay about this situation when I don't know how to feel okay about it myself.

27.

Ms. Ortiz is standing at her podium looking over some papers when I walk in after school on Monday.

She smiles big when she sees me. "Well, this is a nice surprise. Am *I* in trouble?"

I smile back. "No, but I was wondering if you have a few minutes to talk?"

"For you, of course." We sit down in the front row. "What can I do for you, Yvonne?"

"I wanted to ask you about music therapy."

"Oh!" Her face lights up. "Well, I've never been through a program myself, but I'm sure some of my former students would be happy to talk to you about it. One of them is currently studying in the undergrad program at CSUN. She was very happy there the last time we spoke. What is it about music therapy that appeals to you?"

I knew I'd probably have to answer this question, but I still feel shy when I start talking. "When I first started playing, I loved everything about violin. I felt special, like I'd found something I could be really good at. Something I could maybe do forever."

Ortiz nods.

"And my dad...He's great at what he does. One of the best in his industry, so I always felt like I needed to be the best, too. Especially with all the money he was paying Denis for my private lessons and how much we spent on the violin."

"I never got the idea that your father put pressure on you."

"He didn't....He doesn't. But with his work, it seems like there's no in between. There's either perfection or failing, and that's how I started looking at violin. It was the only thing I knew how to do, so I figured I had to be at the top of my game. And that's when I started thinking about conservatories and playing professionally, but I realized that's not what I want. I don't like that sort of stress. I don't like feeling competitive, and to be honest, I don't even feel like I want to perform. I just want to play."

Ortiz's eyes are so warm it's easy to keep going. And the more I talk, the lighter I feel.

"I also realized...I'm alone. A lot. Violin keeps me company." I'm not worried about Ortiz feeling sorry for me, but it is hard to say those words aloud without feeling a bit pitiful. "Playing makes me feel better, and I was thinking... if my music makes *me* feel better, maybe it can make other people feel better, too. People who need it."

"Hence music therapy."

I nod.

"Well, I think your heart is in the right place, which is the first step. Music therapists don't make a lot of money. You'd have to be committed."

"I figured." I shrug. "That's not important.... I want to like what I do."

"You'd have to get board certified after completing your degree. And then you'd find yourself in some challenging situations with your clients. Do you think you'd be up to the task?"

"I think maybe I'd like to try." It feels like a natural progression for me where conservatories never did.

She tilts her head as she looks at me. "Well, I think that's wonderful, Yvonne. I'm proud of you."

I duck my head. "Why?"

"I thought you were going to quit. I had to tell myself that if you made that choice, it was right for you and it wasn't my place to discourage you from doing so. But I'm glad to see you want to stick with it, in your own way. I'd wager that the most fulfilling occupations aren't the most high profile."

I hesitate but decide to continue. I've been so honest with Ortiz up to this point. "Do you think I'd be good enough to teach? Like, teach lessons to kids who've never had them? Not at a school—more like an after-school program."

I keep thinking about the woman at Cooper Youth Center. How she confirmed they had a music program but no one to teach strings. I don't know if they're hiring or if I'd even be qualified, but I'm curious. It would help fill my time. I wouldn't have to be alone so much or rely on Sabina and Warren to keep me company.

"I do. You have the talent and knowledge, Yvonne. The challenge is finding the best way to put it to use."

"I'm not sure music is what I want to do.... I'm considering culinary school, too."

"You cook!"

"I bake."

"A woman of many talents. I salute you," she says with a smile. "I'm not going to tell you which way to go. I have total faith that you will make the right choice for you. You *have* choices. That's the most important thing."

I wish I could capture Ortiz's confidence and bottle it up because I need it. Some choices are easier than others, and I still have the most difficult one ahead of me.

28.

What's the big deal about Holden Caulfield, anyway?" Sabina yawns and tosses her paperback of *The Catcher in the Rye* to the end of the bed. "Can you believe they're still teaching this book?"

"Isn't it supposed to represent the universal theme of adolescent alienation?" I say in the Very Important Voice our literature teacher uses.

"It's boring and outdated." She nudges the book with her toe as she looks up at me. "Sorry we have to be here."

Her moms finally started to complain about how little they've seen her at dinnertime in the past couple of weeks, so she invited me over tonight to eat and do homework.

"I like being here. It's better to be around people lately."

I tap my pencil against the edge of my AP government text-book. "Sabs...do you think they know?"

"Mom and Mama Jess? I swear, I haven't told them."

"I know you haven't. I just feel like they were looking at my stomach."

She pokes my arm. "They weren't looking at your stomach, girl."

"I feel like people are. Like they can tell. Don't mothers have that instinct? Like, they can *sense* another mother?"

"Have you been looking at those mommy blogs?"

I poke her back. "No. I just feel like people have been looking at it lately."

"You're paranoid."

"Well, you're looking at it now."

"Because you're *talking* about it, bozo!"

"*Bozo?*"

We look at each other and burst out laughing at the same time. It feels good. Unfamiliar these days.

She picks at a loose thread on one of the pillows, her smile fading. "Have you decided yet?"

"No. I mean, I don't think I'm ready for a baby, but then lots of people aren't and they make it work."

Sabina nods, her face unreadable.

"But it would be easier to just get it taken care of and go on with my plans like normal. Lots of people do that, too."

Footsteps approach from down the hallway, and Sabina

and I fall silent until Mama Jess knocks and sticks her head in.

"Hey, I forgot about these cookies I picked up after work," she says, holding out a bakery box. "Want some?"

Sabina bounds over, peering into the box. She plucks a giant chocolate chip cookie from inside and breaks off a piece, popping it into her mouth.

Mama Jess smiles at me. "Yvonne?"

I barely ate anything for dinner, so she'll probably think something's up if I decline a cookie. I get up and take one, too. "Thanks."

"I need milk," Sabina says, her mouth full of cookie. She looks at me to see if I want some, but I shake my head.

She disappears down the hallway, leaving me alone with Mama Jess.

I sit on the edge of the bed with my cookie, unsure of what to say. I've never felt self-conscious about being alone with Mama Jess; she's the easiest of Sabina's parents, by far. But it doesn't help that she's a shrink and seems to be able to suck information out of anyone without even trying.

"How have you been, Yvonne?" She leans against the doorframe, balancing the bakery box against her hip. "We haven't seen much of you around here lately."

"I've been good. Just staying busy with school."

If my textbook weren't open behind me, I'm not sure I'd believe that sentence myself. I've been walking around school in a haze. Sometimes I can barely remember that I've done the reading and have no recollection of completing the assignments I hand in.

"Wrapping up your applications? I know Sabina's happy to be done with hers."

"I haven't really decided what I'm going to do yet. I've just had a lot going on."

Mama Jess nods and looks at me for a long moment before she speaks again. "Yvonne, I don't want to overstep any boundaries, because I know you have a father who loves you, but...if there's anything Cora or I could ever do for you, I hope you'll let us know. You've been close to Sabina for a long time, and we're so happy she has a friend like you. We love having you here."

"I'm happy to have a friend like her." I smile at Mama Jess; big, so maybe I can ward off the tears threatening to well up. "And thank you...I'll remember that."

Sabina walks back in then, carrying a glass of milk with half her cookie dunked inside. "What are you guys talking about?"

"How great I am," I say before cramming a bite of cookie into my mouth. It's good—chewy and moist, with a touch of sea salt.

"Guess I have good taste in people." Sabina looks at Mama Jess. "Can you leave that box in here?"

She does and takes a cookie before blowing a good-bye kiss across the room.

I turn to Sabina. "You're sure she doesn't know?"

"I'm sure I didn't tell her. You know she lives on some spiritual plane above the rest of us."

"Sabs, what would you do? If you were in my position?"

She lets out a long, loud breath. "I don't know. I've thought about it, but I don't know."

"I'm practically a walking ad for abstinence before marriage, I guess."

"No," she says firmly. "This isn't punishment for having sex."

I stare at her. "How can you say that when you're so against sex before marriage?"

"I'm against it for me, not you." Sabina sighs. "I wish I'd never said that to you that day...about being worried."

"It was the truth, wasn't it?"

"Yes, but I didn't mean it to sound so judgy. What I meant was that you deserve the best, and I don't want guys taking advantage of you."

"They're not taking advantage of me if I want it as much as they do."

"I know, but I think about Omar and how things could have gone really wrong with him. You don't even know his last name, and he lied to you." She doesn't sound disapproving, just concerned. Like a sister. "You're alone so much, and I keep thinking about that night you took him home.... What if something bad had happened?"

"It didn't," I say softly. Though I've thought of that, too, and how lucky I am that he was only a liar and not something worse. Still, it bugs me, wondering what else he might have lied about. A small consolation is that my STD tests came back negative. The nurse said they wouldn't follow up unless there was an issue, but I still called them to make sure. The relief that washed over me when she said everything was negative was brief but intense. One less thing to worry about.

"I know." Sabina pauses. "Look, I don't want you to think you have to keep things from me because we don't see eye to eye on the whole sex thing."

"Okay. But I don't want to feel like you're judging me. How can you promise you won't do that?"

"I'm not perfect. I can't stop worrying about you just because you tell me to." She picks at a hangnail on her thumb, then stops and looks at me. "But I promise I'll try to remember we can still have wildly different beliefs and be best friends."

"Well, I don't know how much you'll have to worry about." I twist my mouth to the side as I contemplate what I'm about to say. "I don't know how soon I'll want to have sex again."

"Not even with Warren?"

I consider this. I'm unsettled by how we left things at his apartment, but I love Warren. Still...every time I think about having sex, I shudder. Sabina said what happened isn't punishment, yet I can't help feeling that way right now. It feels like I'll never be able to have sex again without thinking I'll get pregnant, no matter how many precautions I take. The nurse at the clinic said this feeling was normal and that it wouldn't last forever.

"Maybe Warren. Maybe sometime in the future."

I'd like to think we can get back to a good place, but I don't know if Warren will get over this. I hope he does. I might not have the energy to keep convincing him I never meant to hurt him.

Sabina nods, then looks down at her hands for a moment before she meets my eyes again. "Did you know there's such a thing as an abortion doula?"

I shake my head.

"They provide support for girls and women getting abortions . . . like the doulas that help during childbirth. But the opposite, I guess."

"Do they do abortions?"

"No. Childbirth doulas don't deliver the babies. Doulas are, like, trained companions. To make the process easier."

"Oh." I never knew something like that existed.

Sabina sets her glass on the nightstand. "I didn't mention it because I don't want you to think I'm trying to tell you what to do."

"I know you're not."

She chews on her lip. "You keep saying how much I'm

helping you by being here, but you help me, too. My life is so structured and planned out, and you remind me that it's okay to be spontaneous sometimes."

"Well, I think we all know I could use a little more structure."

"That's why we balance each other out."

We eat too many cookies and finish our homework, and I think it's strange how there is a difference between being alone and being lonely.

I think about what Warren said, how his father is blood not family. Sabina isn't my blood, but she is my family. Even when I am lonely, I'm never truly alone with her by my side.

29.

I was planning to show up unannounced at Omar's, especially since he's still not answering his phone, but then, out of the blue, he calls. He wants to see me, and I'm relieved when he asks if I can meet him at the house, because at least there will be other people there. I can't believe I had sex with someone I'm now worried about being alone with.

I could have stopped talking to him—deleted his number and avoided the beach for a while. But I still want that closure. It seems necessary; maybe because I've never had closure with the one person who was always supposed to be here. And I want to confront him about his lie.

Someone finally mowed the lawn at the communal

house, but now there's not much lawn to speak of. It's just an expanse of brown, cracked patches; nothing like a proper drought-tolerant yard with neatly landscaped plots of deer grass, succulents, and lavender. I pick my way across the dry earth.

Like last time, the main door is open, and I can see into the living room through the screen. Keely is sitting on the couch, alone. She's staring at her phone, and I guess she didn't hear me walk onto the porch because she doesn't look up at all.

"Um...hi." My voice comes out so small that I clear my throat and start over. "Hi, Keely."

"Door's open," she says without looking up. And when I step inside, she briefly turns to say, "Omar's not home yet."

She's not scowling, but she doesn't bother to smile, either.

"Oh...okay. Should I come back?"

Keely shrugs. "Up to you. You can wait in here if you want."

I haven't been inside the house since the first night I was here. The front room is larger than I realized, and it just looks like a normal—albeit shabby—living room without bodies filling every square inch. Other people are here, their voices floating from different rooms of the house.

Keely is barefoot, wearing pilled yoga pants and a cropped T-shirt. Her face is free of makeup, and she looks younger than every other time I've seen her.

"He had to run an errand, and it's taking longer than he thought," she says. "He should be back soon."

It would have been nice if he'd called to let me know that himself. "Thanks for letting me wait in here."

She shrugs again. "Sure. I'm going upstairs to practice."

She bounds up the stairs on the balls of her feet, and I perch on the edge of the dumpy couch, trying not to think about the questionable stains and where it was before it ended up here. Even the walls in this house are dingy.

A couple of people walk through the room as I wait, nodding or waving hello like they know me. How could you even keep track of who's supposed to be here and who's not when so many people are living here?

Suddenly, the sweet, sad notes of Keely's viola wind their way down the stairs. I sit up and listen, trying to figure out what she's playing. I recognize the music. Mozart, I think, but I can't remember the name of the piece. I want to hear more, because she and Omar have only played contemporary when I've seen them on the beach, and the jam session was improvised.

I stand and move closer to the stairs. I still can't hear as well as I'd like. I don't know if I'm supposed to be upstairs— Omar didn't show me the second floor when he gave me a tour that first night. I look around, but no one is watching. I slowly walk up the staircase, following the sound of her viola. The notes lead me to a door at the end of the hallway.

246

It's cracked open, and I peek through the sliver of space. Keely is standing next to a window, playing with her eyes closed.

I remain outside the room for the rest of the movement. Until the last note fades and she relaxes, holding the instrument and bow by her side.

And then she turns and looks right at me through that crack in the door.

Fuck.

I back away, mortified, but she flings the door open before I can move down the hallway.

"Can I help you?" It reminds me of the first day I talked to Omar, only his voice was kind. Friendly. Keely sounds like she's talking to the shitty neighbor kid who won't leave her alone.

"Sorry." I twist a thick band of braids around one hand. "I'm not trying to be a creep; I just wanted to hear you better. You're so good."

"Thanks."

"Was that Mozart?"

"Yeah." Her voice is flat but she looks at me curiously. "How long have you been playing?"

"A while now...eleven years."

"Oh. I didn't know that."

I nod, trying to think of something to say that would prove how much I know about music. As I'm searching for the right words, I look over her shoulder to the open doorway. "Is this your room?"

"Yeah."

"The one you share with Omar?"

I can't read her look. Surprise that I knew they shared a room? Embarrassment that she has to talk about it with me?

"That's the one," she says.

From what I can see, it's plain and cramped, with a couple of music stands, sheet music everywhere, a shabby bureau against the wall, a window that needs to be cleaned, and a bed.

A bed. *One* bed.

Omar explicitly told me they didn't share one, but I don't see a pallet or a sleeping bag on the floor. He lied again.

That's when I recognize the look in Keely's eyes: pity.

"Sorry to bother you," I mumble before heading back to the stairs. I have to get out of here. I'm not going to stick around and see what else he's lied about.

"Wait." As much as I want to leave, Keely's voice makes me stop. "What are you guys?"

I turn around. "Nothing."

"Does he know that?"

"He left for two weeks and didn't tell me. And him sharing a bed with you is the second thing he's lied to me about. I was going to tell him tonight...that I don't want to see him anymore. That I don't trust him."

"Well. I probably shouldn't be saying this, but...you dodged a bullet."

"What?"

She purses her lips. "Omar is—I've never met anyone like him. He has, like, this magnetic pull, but he's not someone you want to be attached to."

I frown. "You two do everything together."

"Look...I love him. I probably always will. But he's unrealistic. He has all these plans and—I know this sounds harsh, but he's not as good as he thinks he is. We've gone on a ton of auditions together, and I'm the only one they ever want for the gig. He went on tour with me because he really thought they were going to suddenly decide they needed both of us and not just me. He thinks he can get by on his charm and good looks, but it hasn't worked yet."

I didn't know that. He's emphasized how much they're a team that I assumed they were on the same level. But now that I think about it, I've never really heard him play by himself. And even during his solo parts, when he's playing with Keely, I've always been more drawn to her talent. It seems to course right through her, like she's not even trying.

"There's one more thing," she says after a pause. "He's not exactly who he says he is."

"Yeah, I know. He told me he works at a youth center downtown, and they've never heard of him."

"He's still using that tired old lie?" She shakes her head,

249

then absentmindedly squeezes a hand around her Afro puff. "Did he tell you about how we got to this house?"

"He said you stayed in shelters and homeless camps....Is that not true?"

"That's true," she says. "But it didn't have to be. I had to get away from my asshole dad, but Omar's parents have money. Like, a lot. They sent him to Berklee, and then when he dropped out and said he didn't want to go back to school, they cut him off."

My mouth drops open. "What?"

"He's a trust fund kid. And he'd have all that money if he stopped living like some hipster bum, but he's too prideful. He even changed his name once he got out here."

I can't say anything. I feel sick.

"His real name is Grant, but he thought it sounded too white...too *privileged.* So he started going by Omar. I only found out after I saw his license a few months after we'd been living together." She hesitates. "To be honest, maybe that's another reason I can't seem to get away from him. It feels safe, knowing he has something to fall back on if he gets his shit together. And he still gets money from his family. That's the only reason we're not still on the streets. One of his older brothers felt bad for him and started funneling him money in secret."

"This is all true?"

"I wouldn't lie about this," she says. "I love him, but I don't like him sometimes. I don't want you to think you missed out on some great catch."

There's something I need to ask her because I want to know the whole truth. It's uncomfortable, but I forge ahead. "Were you guys still sleeping together when he and I were seeing each other?"

"No," she says in a firm voice. "We only hook up when neither of us is with someone else."

"And you believe he's honest with you?"

Her eyes narrow. "I think we're done here. I've already told you too much."

That's fair. "I'm glad you said something. . . . I thought you hated me."

"You seem like an okay person. I think you deserve to know." She appraises me for a moment. "I can't hate you. I don't even know you."

Downstairs, the screen door slams. "Keely?" he calls out. "Is Yvonne here?"

The sound of his voice makes me furious.

Keely raises her eyebrows as if to say good luck before she retreats to their room.

Omar greets me with a huge grin from his post at the bottom of the staircase. "Hey, sorry I'm late. Got held up running an errand and the train was late and—"

"I went down to the Cooper Youth Center," I say when I'm standing in front of him. "They said you don't work there. They've never even heard of you."

I expect his face to go slack with remorse, but if there's anything he's better at than violin, it's lying. "What? I've worked there for a while now. Maybe the person you talked to was new."

"She's not new, and I'm not stupid. Is there anything I know about you that's true? Were you ever going to tell me you share a *bed* with Keely?"

"Oh, that." He waves his hand in the air. "We're roommates, nothing more."

"That's another lie, and you know it." My neck and face are getting hot.

Finally, his shoulders drop in defeat. "Come on, Yvonne. So I slipped up. It's not a big deal." He moves closer to me. "It doesn't change how we feel about each other...or our chemistry."

He slips his hands around my waist. I slap them away. He's so shocked that he moves back, and I take that opportunity to step around him so he's no longer standing in my path to the door.

"I don't want to see you again. Delete my number."

He shakes his head, chuckling. "Guess I was wrong about you being so mature for your age. You high school girls act so goddamn virtuous, but you didn't think twice about fucking me, did you?"

I am shaking with fury, but my words come out cool as ice.

"I never pretended to be anything I'm not, but I know I don't trust a fucking thing you've told me. Did you really leave Berklee or did they kick you out? It's not like you're anywhere near as talented as Keely is... *Grant.*"

I don't stick around to see if the guilt finally shows.

I deliberately slam the door behind me and walk across the dying lawn of that dying house for the last damn time.

30.

When I asked my father if we could have dinner together, he seemed startled.

He relaxed a little when I suggested we eat at the restaurant, that I could come by after they'd closed. I figured it was best to talk to him in the place he loves most, but I couldn't bear the thought of talking about something so serious and personal in his cramped, sterile office.

Luckily, Warren is off the night I go to the restaurant. We've texted a few times since our dinner, but we haven't seen each other, and I think that's best. He's anxious to know my decision, and I wonder if it's killing him, not being able to talk to my dad about something so big.

I wait for my father at a table up front. It's not a high-top, but it reminds me of the nights I used to do my homework in Lou's restaurant. The dining room is almost empty; a couple sits in the corner, lingering over coffee and panna cotta.

My heart won't stop pounding. I know I don't have to do this. I have enough money saved up that if I choose to have an abortion, I won't need his help. But I know I can't leave here tonight without telling him. Maybe I just want some real emotion from him. Or maybe this is a test—to see how he'll react when I tell him I did one of the few things he said would upset him. I can't help wondering if he'll be so angry, so disappointed in me, that he might stop loving me.

The restaurant has an open kitchen, so I can watch Dad working. He's calmer toward the end of the night; he takes his time as he moves between the stations instead of zipping through like he's running a race, and he seems considerably more patient with his staff.

Once the stragglers have paid and left, my father comes over to get me. "Ready? I thought we'd eat over there, since it's close to the kitchen."

I follow him to the table, the one Warren once told me is the best in the restaurant. Bottles of flat and sparkling water sit in the center, and a basket of fresh bread is placed between our plates. He's treating this like it's a real meal, like I'm someone important, and it touches me so much that tears prick at the corners of my eyes. I don't want him to look at me differently after this. Maybe things aren't great between us now, but I don't want them to change for the worse.

"Okay now," he says, coming back from the kitchen with the first plate. He sits down, still in his chef coat. "First up: fried chicken liver salad."

He serves me first and I dig right in, making sure there's a piece of crispy liver on every forkful of greens. "This is so good," I say before I've even finished chewing. Thank God my appetite is back, at least for this evening.

"You like it?"

"Yeah, is it new?"

"It is. And I'm glad to see you scarfing it down because you hated chicken livers when you were a little girl."

"I did?" I look down at my plate, shocked that I could ever hate anything that tastes this good.

"*Hated.* They weren't fried, so I'll give you that. But I tried to feed them to you with dinner one night, and you spit them out. Right on your place mat." He laughs a little—a chuckle, almost. "That's the only food I can remember you not liking."

"Really?"

He swallows his bite. "Oh, yeah. You liked some things more than others, of course, but you've always been easy with food. Never a picky eater. You get that from me, you know."

"Obviously." But that makes me wonder if my mother was picky. I shove another bite of salad into my mouth so I won't be tempted to ask. He seems to be in a good mood, and I need to preserve that for as long as I can.

"So, what's the occasion?" he says, gesturing to the table. To us purposely spending time together.

"Can—can we wait until dessert?"

He squints at me. "That bad, huh?"

"Maybe I just want to enjoy your food."

"Mmhmm." But he appeases me and asks how school is going, which leads to talk about college applications. And for the first time since I've started thinking about what to do after I graduate, I feel good discussing my choices.

"I've been researching music therapy programs."

"Music therapy, huh? So you're sticking with the violin after all." He doesn't seem to think it's a good or a bad idea. He just sounds thoughtful.

"Maybe."

"Well, Lou told me about his offer. Is that an option for you?"

I take a long drink of water. "Maybe, but...I never thought about being a pastry chef. Do you think I'm good enough?"

"I think you surprised the hell out of me with how talented you are," he replies. "And that's without any training."

My face burns at his approval.

He gets up to take the salad plates back to the kitchen and returns with the entrée: ricotta-filled ravioli with caramelized figs, prosciutto, and rosemary. "Something a little lighter, after all those chicken livers."

Dad continues after he serves himself. "Yvonne, I know it's a big leap, deciding what you're going to do after high school...or what you *think* you're going to do. But nothing is guaranteed. I took a chance on this place and, honestly, I lucked out. About sixty percent of restaurants fail in the first year, and eighty percent within the first five years. You don't think I was terrified that I'd have to go crawling back to Lou for help? Or worse, for a job?"

"But you *love* what you do. I like baking—I really like it. But it doesn't feel like what I was *born* to do."

"Some people don't figure out what they were meant to do until later in life," he says. "Some start out doing what they thought they wanted and realize it's not at all what they should be doing. It's a journey, and you can't expect yours to look like anyone else's."

I try to make my pasta last as long as possible. I'm aware that with every bite of ravioli, the closer I am to sharing my secret. To ruining this nice evening we're having. I'm practically shaking by the time he takes our plates away and returns with panna cotta for us to share. I don't even pretend that I'm going to eat it, and when I glance up, my father is sitting down, looking at me. Waiting.

I open my mouth, but nothing comes out. I take a quivering drink of water and try again. Nothing.

"Are you pregnant?"

I stare at him, swallowing hard. "How did you...?" I look down at my stomach to see if I somehow didn't realize I'm showing, but it's still flat as ever. It's still too early for that.

"Just a guess. Oh, Yvonne." He doesn't sound disappointed. Just tired. Like he doesn't have the energy to even engage with something like this right now. Or ever. He doesn't hesitate at all before he asks, "Is it Warren's?"

"Did he tell you?" He promised he wouldn't, but then Warren has always been weakest where my dad is concerned.

"He hasn't said a word."

"I don't—I don't know whose it is." No matter how many times I say this, I don't think I'll ever stop feeling like I'm hearing someone else speak instead of myself. "Either Warren or... there was another guy. We hung out for a while."

"You're sure you're pregnant? You're not just late?"

"I'm sure. And I was safe, but I guess nothing is one hundred percent."

"Well." Dad takes a drink of coffee, then leans forward on his elbows. I swear, deep bags just appeared under his eyes in the last two minutes. "Mistakes happen. I'll give you money to take care of it."

"What if I don't want to take care of it?" I'm not sure what the right decision is, but I know I don't want him making it for me.

His face sets into a deep scowl. "Don't be foolish, Yvonne.

You're in no position to take care of a baby right now. You just sat here and told me you don't even know what to do with your life."

"What if being a mom is the answer?" I don't know that it is, but I am feeling stubborn. And upset. That I don't have a mother to discuss this with, that my father is so willing to make this decision for me when he has no idea what it's like to be me.

"You really think your calling is to be a teenage mother?" He shakes his head, looking at the bottle of sparkling water. "I raised you to know you can be more than that."

"No, you raised me to learn how to be alone all the time."

He looks at me. "What are you talking about?"

"You are *never* around. And when you are, there's always someone else with us, like Warren or Lou."

"You know that's the nature of my job. That's what puts food on the table and what paid for all those violin lessons over the years. I have to work, Yvonne."

"I'm lonely." The words don't come easily, but I force them out. "I hate that I have to eat dinner alone and that you're never up to see me off to school. I hate that you being successful means I miss out on having a full-time father."

He swallows. "I know I haven't been a perfect dad, but I've tried to make sure you were on the right path. Having a baby when you graduate high school isn't the right path. I don't want you to become another statistic."

"Why do people never say anything about 'statistics' to white kids? I'm a statistic if I have an abortion and a statistic if I have a baby. Black kids don't even get a chance to *think* about doing something wrong before everyone's telling us how vital it is that we don't mess up."

"You know what I mean."

"No, I don't. What would people say if they knew you basically spend every waking moment of your day stoned?"

He throws his napkin on the table. "That has never once hindered my career or my ability to take care of you. It's nobody's business but my own."

"And this is *my* business. I'm eighteen. I don't need your approval for what I do with my body."

"No, but you need my roof over your head. How are you going to take care of a baby with no job and no place to live?"

"So you'd kick me out if I have it. Is that what you're saying?"

He ignores the question. "And who's going to help you take care of it, huh? This other guy, whoever he is? Because I know for damn sure Warren Engel is not ready to be a father."

He runs a hand over his face, and I know he's at his breaking point, but I can't quit talking.

"Did Mom leave because she didn't want to take care of me?"

"Yvonne, stop."

"Was it because of me? Is that why she left? I deserve to

know." Tears that have been pent up for years are streaming down my face by this point, but I don't wipe them away.

"Please stop."

"Do you wish she'd had an abortion?"

"Yvonne, that is *enough*." He's standing now, glaring at me. "You are better than this—*smarter* than this. I will not stand by and watch you ruin your life when you could have a perfectly good education and career ahead of you."

"I wouldn't be like her," I whisper. "I wouldn't just up and leave."

"You need to go home." He turns his back to me. "Go to bed, and we'll talk about this when you've had some rest."

I open my mouth to respond, but there's nothing else to say. He's said exactly what he thinks, and there's no arguing with him when his mind is made up like this.

I've rarely seen him so mad, and I know it's partly because I brought up my mother.

I also know that he didn't tell me I was wrong when I asked if I am the reason she's gone.

31.

There's a text waiting for me from Warren when I get out of my last class the next day. He's outside—well, waiting outside school grounds.

I slowly walk toward his car on the street, preemptively dreading what's going to happen between us. I'm feeling even worse after talking to my father. Every time I replayed our conversation today, I wanted to shrivel up into my seat and disappear. Go back to bed and sleep until I forget about everything.

I get into the passenger seat and we stare at each other for a while in uncertain silence.

"I'm sorry," Warren finally says. "I was a dick to you and . . . I'm sorry. Turns out I'm pretty bad at this stuff."

"I don't think anyone's good at it."

"Can we talk?"

"I'm here."

"I mean, can we go somewhere?"

So we drive. I don't tell him where to go, and he doesn't say where he's going. I don't think he knows. We end up at a little diner in Hollywood. It's so nondescript that I wonder if it's one of those places that looks super-average but is actually iconic among longtime residents, known for the best cheese-burger or onion rings or guacamole.

But I don't see any faded signs declaring it the number one anything when we walk in, and the menu offers the average diner fare. We both order coffee. I get a basket of waffle fries, and Warren asks for a slice of banana cream pie.

"This was my first job," he says, looking around at the scuffed walls. They're covered in framed, faded headshots autographed with thick black marker by celebrities. I don't recognize most of them.

"You worked here?"

He nods. "As a fry cook. When I was in high school. From sophomore year to when I graduated. I staged at Lou's restaurant, then I got a job with your dad."

"Did you like it?" It feels strange making small talk with Warren, but the only alternative is to dive right into what we didn't finish the other night, and I'm not looking forward to that.

"It was a job. People didn't care about food here like they do where I am now. But they were nice. And I consider it part of my training....I just never thought at the time that I'd be where I am now."

"You like where you are now?"

"I love working with Sinclair. I'm sure I'll want to open up my own place someday, but for now, this feels right." He pauses, his eyes on the table. "I've been thinking a lot about where I am lately, and I don't know if I'm ready for a baby, Yvonne."

I let out a long breath. I'm glad he said it right away. At least now I don't have to suffer through the rest of the afternoon harboring this immense dread.

The server drops off our food. Neither of us moves until he leaves, and we don't touch our food, either.

"I'm not gonna lie—I was really pissed that you slept with that other guy," Warren says in a careful voice. "I know I fucked up, and I know that we weren't *together* together. But...God, it was like my heart *hurt* when you told me. It felt physical."

I fold down a corner of the parchment paper that lines the fry basket, making a tiny triangle. "I'm not sorry for sleeping with him, because I didn't do anything wrong. But I'm sorry I hurt you. And...I'm sorry that I don't know whose it is. I know that complicates this whole thing."

"I love you." He's looking right at me now. "You are one

of my favorite people in the world. If I thought I could be a good dad right now, I'd want to have a baby with you. Like, no questions asked. Hell, I'd probably even raise some other guy's kid if it meant I could be with you."

I want to look away, because his words are creating a storm of emotions inside me and I want it to stop. I know that where he's going with this won't necessarily be what I want to hear, but he's being honest with me. Speaking from the heart. I can't fault him for that, so I keep staring into his tea-colored eyes.

"Ever since you told me, I've been thinking of all the ways we could make it work. And maybe we could. I don't want anyone but you." He sighs. "But then I think...what if I end up being a shitty father like my dad was?"

"You'd never run off like that, Warren."

"No, but there are other ways to be a bad father. I'm worried I wouldn't know how to be a good one since I've never had one. And...I guess I can't help wondering how I'd really feel if we found out the kid wasn't mine. I'd still love them, but what if I never stopped resenting the fact that I wasn't the biological dad?"

"You wouldn't do that, either," I say softly.

He shakes his head. "I think people believe there are a lot of things they wouldn't do, and then they surprise themselves when shit gets tough. Maybe that was my dad's problem—your mom's, too."

I think of last night, how my father never answered my question.

Warren slides his pie plate out of the way, then my fries and coffee cup. He reaches across the table for my hands. I give them to him.

"I'm not telling you what to do," he says. "If you want to keep it, you should. I'm not going to disappear on you as a friend. I can at least be here for you that way. And maybe more—who knows? But I wanted to be honest with you about how I'm feeling. I just think...love isn't always enough, you know?"

"I told my dad. He knows it could be yours."

Warren's face pales, then deepens to a bright shade of pink. "Is he going to murder me?"

"Murder might be a bit extreme. Anyway, I think I'm the one he's really pissed at. He wants me to get an abortion, and he wouldn't entertain any other options."

"You know Sinclair. He's so sure he's always right, but he comes around eventually."

"I don't think so, Warren." I swallow. "He was about some serious tough love. I don't think he'd let me stay in the house if I kept it. He's so goddamn worried about what people would think."

"It doesn't matter what he thinks," Warren says. "Or anyone else. It's your decision. You have to do what's right for you."

I stare down at my lap. Trying to have a baby on my own would be too hard. People do it, but what if I couldn't handle it? And what if I'm still so fucked up from my mother that I'd be a terrible parent, like Warren thinks he might be? I'd try my best, I know it, but I'm not sure I'm ready for that kind of pressure. If I have a baby, I'm not giving it up to anyone else, and if I have an abortion... My father says he doesn't dwell on the past, but I don't know if I have that gene. What if I always wish I'd had the baby instead?

"I don't know what the right thing is, Warren."

He drops my hands and I look up at him, wounded. But he's getting up from his seat and coming over to my side of the booth so he can sit with me. I lean my head on his shoulder and he puts his arms around me. We sit like that, together and saying nothing, long after our coffee gets cold.

I'm in such a deep, deep sleep later that night that when my father shakes me awake, I sit straight up, gasping for air.

"It's just me, Yvonne," he says. He's standing in front of my nightstand, blocking most of the light from the lamp he turned on.

I check the clock on the wall. A quarter past one. "What's wrong?" I mumble.

"She left because of me."

That shocks me into consciousness. "What?"

"Your mother." His voice is gruff. "She left because I told her to."

I stare at him, lips parted. "Why would you tell her to leave? Why would you *do* that? She was my *mother*."

"She didn't love me," he says. "Well, she did, at first. And then I started working too much. I wanted to provide for the two of you...my girls....She said she'd rather be poor than never see me. I loved her. A lot. But I loved my work too much."

"So she just left?"

"She threatened a few times, and finally, I told her if she was going to do it, she should just go." His eyes are glassy in the lamplight. "One day I came home and she was gone. She didn't leave a note, and her family wouldn't talk to me. I've done everything short of hire a private detective to find her. I just want to know if she's okay. But there's no electronic footprint. She doesn't want to be found."

I swallow. "So why didn't she take me with her?"

His face falls. "I can't answer that, Yvonne. I...I suppose it was easier to disappear without a child in tow. I've always wondered...."

"What?" I prompt him.

He breathes in deeply through his nose. "I've always wondered if there was someone else...but it doesn't matter. I didn't treat her the way she deserved to be treated, and I'm sorry for that. I'm sorry for how it affected you."

I think about mentioning the man by the apple bins all those years ago, but as I look at my father's sad, tired eyes, I stop myself. It wouldn't change anything. She still left. She still didn't care enough about her own child to take me with her.

"There's something I think you should have," he says, and from behind his back, he pulls out a photo.

I rub my eyes and take it from him. I've seen only a couple of pictures of my mother. Years ago, I asked why there weren't more, and he said she didn't like photos. That she preferred to live in the moment instead of documenting every second of her life.

The picture is of me and her. I'm sitting in a high chair with a tiny cake in front of me. A giant candle in the shape of the number one is planted in the middle of the chocolate frosting. I'm cheesing for the camera with a halo of black curls on my head and drool running down my chin to my bib. She's gazing at me. Her smile is subtle, but her eyes are aglow. With so much love, it makes my chest constrict. It makes my lungs feel as if they have collapsed, as if I can't get any air.

"I've kept this to myself all this time because I didn't want you to feel any worse about her leaving," he says. "She loved you more than anything in this world, Yvonne. Wholeheartedly."

And I know now, that at some point, she wanted me.

Maybe it was the wrong decision to have me. Maybe she changed her mind a million times about what she wanted *after* she had me. But all my memories, vague as they are, are real. She did the best she could while she was here. She loved me.

"I've spent all this time wishing she had never gone away," I say. "It sucks growing up without a mom. I hate not knowing what that's like."

"I know, Yvonne." His face is so stricken, I wonder if he's going to cry. I've never seen my father so much as shed one tear.

"But...I don't know. If she didn't want to be a mother or wife anymore...maybe the best thing she ever did was leave me with you."

"Oh, baby girl," he says, his voice thick.

Baby girl. He never calls me that. I look up at him in wonder.

"I know I don't say it enough—maybe I've never said it— but I don't know how I would have gone on if she'd taken you with her. I am so, so happy you're here." He runs a hand roughly over the top of my head, a rare display of affection. Then he clears his throat. "I still think you having a baby right now is a bad idea, but I'm not going to put you out on the streets if that's what you choose. We'll figure out a way to make things work. That's what we've been doing all these years, right?"

I sit up on my knees and reach out my arms to hug him—something even more rare in our relationship. He's stiff at first. Not used to this. But he softens, more and more each second. Then he's hugging me back, so tight I think he might never let me go.

32.

Sabina and Mama Jess flank me on either side as we walk up to the front door.

"Are you okay?" Mama Jess says before we go in, smiling at me.

After that night at Sabina's, I started thinking about the abortion doula. And how Mama Jess said she and Cora were there for me if I ever needed anything. I didn't want a stranger to be with me during the procedure, but I wanted to be with people I trust.

I spent the night at their house, and the three of us rode over together to the clinic this morning. Cora had to go into the office but she gave me a big hug and a kiss before she left and told me she loved me. I haven't said much since I got up and showered. Mama Jess set out a light breakfast of fresh fruit and yogurt and croissants. I wasn't supposed to eat anything from midnight on, but I wasn't hungry anyway.

"I think so," I answer Mama Jess, focusing on her fingers wrapped around the door handle.

"Do you need anything before we go in?" she asks gently. "We can take a few minutes, if you want."

"No, I'm okay," I say, trying to return her smile.

I check in at the front desk and then we sit down to wait, again with me between the two of them. Sabina hasn't said much this morning, either, but she's never once looked like she doesn't want to be here with me.

I glance quickly around the waiting room, averting my eyes before they can meet anyone else's. It's pretty early, so there are a just a couple of other women in here. One looks a few years older than me, and the other is older than that, closer to Mama Jess's age. The younger one has a guy with her; the older woman is alone. Neither of them looks as nervous as I feel.

I know this is the right choice, one that I made myself. Yet I feel like I should be more upset about it. Like I should be mourning a baby I'll never know. But the truth is that I don't feel attached to what's in me right now. It doesn't feel like anything more than a bunch of undeveloped cells.

The front door opens. I don't look over until Sabina touches my arm and quietly says, "Yvonne."

I look up to find myself staring at my father.

He says hello to Mama Jess and Sabina as he walks over. Mama Jess moves to give him her seat, and he and I are still looking at each other, silent.

Finally, I speak. "What are you doing here?"

"I, ah, thought I'd just…come down here and be with you. If that's okay," he says quickly, pressing his hands against his knees. He looks over at Mama Jess. "I know you have support, but…"

"I am so, so happy you're here," I say, repeating his words from the other night.

He looks relieved. And a little touched.

When the nurse comes out and calls my name, I feel all of their eyes on me.

"Ready?" Mama Jess says, her kind eyes searching mine.

"Yes." I punctuate it with a nod, just to be clear.

Sabina is leaning forward. She smiles and mouths *I love you.*

My father looks at me, then back at the nurse before he meets my eyes again. "I'll be here when you get out, Yvonne."

"Okay," I say softly.

"I'll be right here," he says again.

This is just one morning, one gesture. But it feels solid

and fresh. Like the start to something new between us. And I think maybe my father and I are going to be okay.

Maybe I'll always wonder what if. Maybe everyone does, no matter what choice they make. But I hope I never regret doing what was right for me at the time.

I hope I'll always be proud of listening to myself.

Acknowledgments

I am grateful to all the people behind the scenes who help me publish books that I'm proud of.

Immense gratitude to my editor Alvina Ling for letting me write the story that was in my heart, and for offering encouragement and guidance that refined it for the page. And to my editor Nikki Garcia, you are a force: Thank you for instantly understanding Yvonne and her world, and for your insightful notes during edits.

I am indebted to the entire team at Little, Brown Books for Young Readers. In particular, thank you to Kheryn Callender, Victoria Stapleton, Jenny Choy, Kristina Pisciotta, Jane Lee, Elizabeth Rosenbaum, Marisa Finkelstein, and Marcie Lawrence for your kindness, dedication, and support through every stage of publication.

To my treasured literary agent, Tina Wexler: Thank you for being my voice of reason, nonstop advocate, trusted friend, and one of the hardest working people in the biz. I admire you greatly.

Jen Simone! I'm eternally grateful to you for letting me pick your brain about the world of violin. You are such a talent and inspiration in your field.

So much love and gratitude to the friends who support and listen to me, read early drafts, and cheer me on through the good times: Kristen Kittscher, Corey Ann Haydu, Lauren Strasnick, Robin Benway, Maurene Goo, Stephanie Kuehn, Sarah McCarry, Lesley Arimah, Elissa Sussman, and Courtney Summers. You all make this solitary writing life a little less lonely and a lot more fun; I appreciate you all.